Mercies of the Fallen

American Civil War Brides: Book 2

Eileen Charbonneau

Print ISBNs
Amazon Print 978-0-2286-1310-7
LSI Print 978-0-2286-1311-4
B&N Print 978-0-2286-1312-1

BWL Publishing Inc

Books we love to write ...
Authors around the world.

http://bwlpublishing.ca

Dedication

*For Deborah and our beautiful friendship, with thanks and
love*

Chapter 1

September 18, 1862
Sharpsburg, Maryland

The bridge over Antietam Creek had three spans in a classic Roman arch design. Its beauty was now pockmarked with cannon shot. Jonathan Kingsley watched it rise out of the battle mist. He wanted to escape this sea of bodies, escape the raven-like clergy sprinkling holy water while raggedy Negros gathered up pieces of men. But his sister was leading him on.

Her skirts wet with the bloodied creek, she leaned over a downed soldier with a massive head wound. Three stripes at his shoulder of his exotic Zouave uniform distinguished him among the dead.

"'Tis powerful dark, Missus," he whispered.

Blind and dying. Leave this one be. But she swept black hair from his forehead. "Do you mind the dark?" she asked.

"Mind it? Only that it has put a cramp in me catching a rat for breakfast, which I'll gladly share with such a fine lady as yourself."

Jonathan reached for his sister's shoulder, to ease her away. Then she made a sound he had not heard since they were children.

Laughter.

The soldier's powder-burned fingers found her skirts, shook them playfully.

"Amuse you, do I? Enough to take me in?"

She took his hand in hers.

"You'll not regret it," he promised.

Jonathan felt suddenly fired with purpose.

"I believe she is regretting it already, Sergeant."

He lifted the soldier, a bigger man than himself, but somehow not heavy. Was he made of straw? "Come on, then," he called. His sister followed.

* * *

Rowan Buckley caught the scent of stored-for-the-winter corn. Where was he? Where was Marie Madeline? Where were her sisters? His mind fought to make sense of place, of time. No, no, he was no longer a child, hiding in the Maries' barn after his escape from Grosse Isle. And the laughing woman was not who he'd taken her for: one of the Marie sisters.

Think, he commanded through the blistering pain. His company's orders were to drive Lee's army back into Virginia. Rowan remembered a stone bridge. He had kept his men low, protected by the thickness of the span. Then, the rest of it came back.

Holy Mother of God. How was he alive? A chill suddenly rattled his teeth. The cannon's blast. Flying. Landing hard. And now. He reached up and felt bandaging around the pain in his head. Around his eyes.

Rowan reached out into the black darkness.

A hand gripped his.

"Where did she go? What did I say to her? I meant no offense." He did not like how young, how desperate he sounded to his own ears.

"How do you know she has left us?" a calm man's voice asked.

"Her scent is gone."

"Scent?"

"Lemon balm. I apologize for my slowness of mind, sir."

"You are anything but slow, my friend. And you made my sister laugh. That is a miracle here."

6

"And where is here?"

"A barn. Now a way station in Hell."

Hell, aye. A good word for the war Rowan had been so eager to join that he'd defied the Maries, who had never been anything but good to him. Away from his regrets. Think. Had he not carried enough of his own wounded behind battle lines? Field hospitals were all set up the same, in three stations: for the ones to be patched and sent back; for those with shattered limbs, waiting for amputations; and for the hopeless-- set aside, waiting for death. In which station was he? You are the dim one, Rowan Buckley, he scolded himself. No one's going to amputate your head.

He swallowed. All right, then. Might as well be useful. "My pack? Is it here?" he whispered.

"Yes."

"And inside, is there a sort of flute… of tin?"

He heard the man going through his belongings. Lightly, as a friend, not a thief would. But that voice had the soft slow cadence of the Southland enemy.

"Here you are, Sergeant," the man announced, closing Rowan's fingers around his penny whistle. The familiar feel of it settled him, helped calm the chattering of his teeth.

"Is there anything else I can do for you, Sergeant?"

The laughing woman's brother would be leaving then? It was all right. Rowan had the whistle, reminding him of who he was.

"Nothing. Thank you, sir. And kindly extend my thanks to the lady, if you would."

"Listen," the voice urged, close to his ear. "You are among the dying."

"I know, sir."

"But you must survive."

"And why is that? Is your sister needing someone to keep her in good humor, maybe?"

How had he said such a brazen thing? But the man laughed. Until the laugh splintered by a shell landing, exploding. Close. Rowan did not need sight to know that.

The man's body covered him. Rowan smelled starched gentleman's cuffs. This was wrong, a civilian protecting him.

"Look to your sister, man," he admonished.

The floorboards shook, the smell of sulfur intensified. Was General McClellan after the retreating rebel army? Were he and his fellow casualties and their angels of mercy now caught in the crossfire? Voices rose in the many American accents he'd come to know over the course of his enlistment.

There, among them: the woman's scent, followed by her voice.

"Jonathan! The walking wounded are leaving us. It will be worse for them outside."

Rowan listened as the man named Jonathan fought for attention against the sounds of rising panic. "Stop, please!" he called out. "The armies will realize their mistake in targeting us! The bombardment will cease. Come back inside—"

"Not me."

"Me neither."

"Give us canteens, muskets. We'll take our chances on the road."

The stench of smoke, of unwashed bodies, wafted around Rowan now. Damned fools. He reached out towards the lemon balm scent. "Please, Missus. Help me to stand."

The woman took his hand. Hers was cool, dry. Good, calm lass. He leaned on her strength, got to his feet.

"Soldiers!" he called out, causing the pain in his head to intensify. But he felt her resolve. She would not allow him to fall. "At attention, every sorry one of you! You will remain here, out of the way!"

Silence.

"Now, sit!" he shouted.

More silence, then "Aye, Sergeant" and "We're sitting, sir."

"My," the woman whispered.

He squeezed her hand. "'Tis the stripes," he confided.

No laughter this time, disappointing him.

"Sergeant, your bandage has gone bloody. You must sit."

"After you tell me your name, Jonathan's sister."

"Ursula."

Another explosion, further away this time. A few shouts. "Easy, you great babies," Rowan warned them.

His fellow wounded apologized. He allowed Jonathan's sister Ursula to help him to his place on the packed ground. She removed, then wound fresh cloth around the pain in his head.

When she was done, he put his whistle to his lips. He began V'la l'bon Vent, the tune Marie Madeline first played as Marie Catherine taught him how to split wood to its rhythms. He thought of Marie Agnes in the doorway with his reward, a tray full of fried beignets smothered in maple syrup. When the bombardment got louder, Rowan switched to the lighthearted slip jig Reaping the Rye.

Ursula had not left his side. She began to clap, keeping its dancing rhythm, like a true Celt. They were in the state of Maryland, where his captain told him Catholics had settled, back when America was a colony of the British. Was she one of his own religion, even if an English-descended one? More hands followed her clapping, and then more. How big was this barn?

Inside his head an itch plagued him, more maddening than the pain. Rowan wondered if there was enough breath in his body to finish. Would it not make a fine story, him dying here, at the end of the tune? Who would tell it? Jonathan's sister Ursula maybe, writing to the Maries, whose farm would run well without him, as it had before his starving, wee-boy's self had stumbled upon it twenty years ago, ready to kill its rats but afraid of the dark, of being alone.

The bombardment grew more distant, then stopped. Time to end with a flourish. The pain was so intense he wanted to cry out. What good would that do? Put your last breath into the instrument.

The tin whistle dropped through his fingers and suddenly his head was in the Ursula's lap. Fine woven wool, folds of it, holding her lemon balm scent.

She unwrapped the bandaging and called for her brother. Rowan felt the man's fingers through the blackness. There was so much blackness.

"Well, Sergeant," he proclaimed, "it appears your whistle has conjured forth an embedded stone."

"The bridge," Rowan whispered, in case they needed that part of the story. "We were blown off the bridge by cannon fire, you see."

Ursula pressed her lips to Rowan's damp forehead. "Good work, getting it out," she approved.

Then they joined together, this brother and sister and himself, in a small conspiracy of laughter.

Rowan wanted, suddenly, not to be the dead hero of a story, even one that would please the Maries. He wanted, like that greedy-for-life child he once was, to hear more laughter. To live.

Chapter 2

Fall 1862

Keedysville, Maryland
October, 1862

Ursula secured her cap for full head movement, guarded her skirts and collar with a full apron, and pinned back her sleeves. As quiet as she was, soft pads joined her footsteps. She smiled down at the mongrel dog that had wandered in after the battle. He rarely barked and was such a solace to the dying that no one had complained of his presence. When they climbed down the back stairs together, it was still before dawn.

Ursula paused at the main floor, where the operating rooms were, and listened. The dog's pointed ears rose, his head tilted in the direction of a stack of neatly folded linens. Yes, she should be able to purloin a half dozen without notice. She put her finger to her lips, although the dog had made no objection, and lifted them off the top of the stack. His short tail, as black and white and scruffy as the rest of him, wagged. He was ready to follow her, as was becoming their pattern, down to the forbidden floor.

They descended the last flight of shorter, narrow stairs to the cellar, the death ward, where the lingering men were already entombed. The dog stayed beside her skirts, not leading her to any of the still forms. Good, she thought. Today's first duty would not be to close eyelids and summon the gravediggers.

Ursula rounded a corner of what had been a laundry room. To her astonishment, Sergeant Buckley sat on the side of his cot, clad only in his long shirt, its rounded tails reaching his knees, its generous sleeves folded back to his elbows. He was shaving himself with great precision, even leaving the short, distinctive tuft of hair under his lip.

Ursula placed her burden on the table beside his bed.

"Might you spare me one of your towels, so I won't leave hairs in today's soup?"

Startled, she bumped her hip against his water basin. The blind are not also deaf, she chastised herself.

"Easy," he soothed, finding her arm after only one futile cast for it.

"I marvel at your ability, Sergeant!"

She watched the eyebrow above his head bandage quirk up. "Ability?"

"To sense my presence."

"'Twas handy for a soldier on night watch duty."

He acknowledged the soft furry body pressed at his knee with a firm stroke. "And a good day to you, my four-legged friend."

"Go visit around," she told the animal who now had a name, thanks to their sergeant. He trotted off to nest beside a sleeping soldier.

Ursula lifted one of the linen towels from her stack and placed it in Sergeant Buckley's open palm. "Shall I marvel on how you attend to your morning ablutions without assistance, then?" Her nervousness made her words sound like frightened birds.

"Hardly a marvel. My fingers still have some dexterity, no?"

"Of course! I mean, without a looking glass."

She felt her cheeks burn. Stupid, stupid. Of what earthly use would a looking glass be to a blind man?

But he merely chuckled and returned to his task. "Oh, I rarely used such a thing, even when sighted."

Her long-ago home had had looking glasses for no purpose other than to reflect light from the tall windows of the receiving foyer. And her dressing table's triple glass could be turned so that she could see both her profile and back. Ursula fumbled into her apron pocket.

"If you are up to a trim of your hair, Sergeant, I would be happy to oblige." She pulled out her scissors, working the blades so he'd know she was ready.

He faced her, smiling slowly. "Now, that would be a grand pleasure."

The rush of delight made her giddy. Ursula pressed her fingers over her widening smile. Did he know it was the only way she could have stayed beside him-- by doing something useful? Of course he did. They had been conspiring together to gain fleeting moments in each other's company since the bloodbath now called the Battle of Antietam.

Battle. Not bloodbath. Remain calm and neutral in this war, she reminded herself of the words of her superiors before she was allowed to use her skills. But how could she remain serene after all she had seen?

As she trimmed Sargent Buckley's black hair's wildness, Ursula watched the thrumming of the vein at his throat. A well-made throat, and unblemished from the bandaged cuts, burns and bruises that a good part of his poor body had endured from the cannon's blast, besides the massive injury to his head.

"Did you sleep well?" she asked quietly.

"Well enough."

An evasion. "And your headaches?"

"Your tea has helped. They are not so bad as before."

Not so bad. But the one doctor who agreed to look at him had only glanced at the terrible wound and muttered, "Matter of time, I'm sorry," before he'd abandoned their sergeant.

Their sergeant? She must stop thinking of him so, as hers and Jonathan's. But had not the doctor done just that? Given him to them? Attention to task, Ursula chided herself. Take more care among the thick curls, so his poor head would not appear plucked.

Still, that was no excuse to sift the strands between her fingers, to linger over the sight of his pale neck or the cords of strength riding up from his back. She saw the muscles clearly though the weave of his nightshirt of homespun linsey woolsey. She'd cleaned his black powder-burned uniform, its lightly woven blue trousers, vest and its short coat with exotic oriental trimmings beside his sergeant stripes.

And when she'd washed the blood from Sergeant Buckley's shirt that first night, she caught the dried lavender scent in its weave. Who had made the shirt for him? He did not speak of home. Nor did ask her to write his goodbyes to a wife, sister, mother. And she did not offer. Was it because she could not bear to think of him belonging to anyone but them, to her and Jonathan? These were childish thoughts, left over from her long-abandoned girlhood. But Ursula remembered that girl. And, over the years she'd learned to love her.

She finished her task and replaced the scissors to her deep side pocket. Never mind. These are blessings, these moments, she decided. Deep blessings, like when their sergeant played his tin whistle.

"Ah now, that feels less cluttered! Did you miss your calling, then?"

"And how do you know I am not a barber, sir?" she teased, dusting his shoulder with a linen towel, leaning down to blow the few clipped hairs from his neck.

He sat higher in response, and he had a soldier's straight bearing already. His voice became a gruff hush. "If you are, I will require a haircut every morning for the rest of my days, if you please."

She laughed. "Oh, you could ill-afford that."

"What's this? Are you saying the United States government cannot pay enough to keep its soldiers well groomed? That borders on treason."

"And it will be your duty to turn me in?"

"My sacred duty, Madame!"

She felt her smile disappear. "Not Madame, Sergeant."

"What then, my dear nursing sister wonder? Might I call you Ursula? Shall I even shorten your name to Sula, maybe? Now that you have seen me at my bath, I mean."

His face colored ruddy, as it had at other times when he seemed concerned that his glib tongue had offended her. It caused the sparks at her intimate places to ignite. Another part of her girlhood. A part that had proved deadly.

The cool cloth in her hand helped not at all. She should not touch it to the tiny soap bubbles clinging to that tuft of hair beneath his lower lip. But she did. The muscle at his cheek twitched.

She should not steal the sharp, startled breath he exhaled. But she tasted that miracle, a given-up-for-dead man's breath: delicious, scented with licorice.

He reached up, finding her waist and lingered there in casual possession, as if they were lovers. Ursula remained still, feeling the heat of his hand through her clothing. Then she leaned closer, took his bandaged head beneath her breasts and closed her eyes, hoping Jonathan would bring more licorice for him today.

"Ursula!"

Speak of the devil, she thought, a phrase she'd learned from the man she was holding close.

"Fetch our sergeant his tin whistle," Jonathan continued. "There is need. Best command that mangy cur of yours as well."

Sergeant Buckley turned toward her brother's voice. "Who?" he asked softly.

"Private Gray," Jonathan answered.

"Fifty-Seventh Maine? Shot through the lungs?"

"Yes."

Ursula waited for Sergeant Buckley to stand on his own, before placing her hand in the crook of his arm. A false gesture, as if he were leading her. "Friend," she called softly to the dog.

"Mother!" she heard the boy cried out from the next room.

"Go on, Sula," Sergeant Buckley whispered, propelling her forward. "Your brother will help me."

She made her feet do what her heart could not bear, except for him and that nudge, except for Friend's head pressing at her knee. She stood still. Private Gray's fingers strafed the air, each breath full of struggle.

"She's here, Charlie," Sergeant Buckley called, behind her. No escape, now.

"You are safe," Ursula said, reaching the cot. She wrapped her arms around his shaking boy's frame. Sergeant Buckley's hand touched her back. Jonathan nodded. Did they know all her doubt, her fears? Did they know what a coward she was?

Their sergeant's music began: soft, joyous; a lilting waltz.

"Is that our own Gus at the fife, Mother?"

"Our very own," Ursula whispered.

"He's got all the squeaks out fine while I been soldiering."

"He has."

"And Barney there, under my arm?"

"Of course."

"Good dog."

The boy stroked Friend's head.

The music kept time with their gentle rocking. Charlie Gray, so far from his mother, looked into her eyes instead. Believing their lies.

The young soldier's ragged breathing gentled, softened, as if he had slipped into a nap. Then, it stopped.

Their ends were all so different. As different as their lives, Ursula supposed, holding him longer than she had to, enjoying being someone's mother long enough for the tune to finish.

"Is Charlie's race run?" Sergeant Buckley spoke into the silence.

"Yes," she answered, collecting the phrase, treasuring it beside his other picturesque questions of their days together, at moments like this one: "Has the lieutenant found his wings, then?" and "Gone into the West to join the greater number of us, has this one?"

Chapter 3

Rowan surrendered his tin whistle to Jonathan, and reached for where he sensed Ursula was, there on the cot, most likely with the boy in her arms. How else could his end have been so peaceful? She took his hand and pressed it to her cheek. Wet with tears. She cried for all of them. Rowan did not want her to cry when it was his turn. He liked that more rare gift, her laughter.

He took a step back, squared his shoulders, and raised his hand to salute. It was nothing official, especially since he outranked the boy who had lived four agonizing days with a punctured lung. Despite all the drilling in the French style he'd mastered with his Zouave unit, Rowan was not a professional soldier. He doubted Private Charlie Gray was old enough to be a soldier at all, so maybe the salute was all right. He heard her dog's soft pad along the dirt floor stop at his knee and realized that Friend was standing at attention beside him.

A door slammed. Clipped footsteps sounded, along with the stench of cigar smoke.

"Nurse. Sister! You must leave these to God. I need a patient readied for surgery. Kindly follow me."

Rowan heard the rustle of her skirts as she rose from the bed.

"Which one are you?" the voice barked at her.

"Ursula, Doctor."

Her footfalls were smothered by the surgeon's heavier ones. The dog leaned against Rowan's legs, growling softly. So, the wee animal did have a voice.

More activity around him left Rowan dizzy and confused. He was in the way, but without guidance. Where was the cellar's stone wall? It would help him stand. Where was Jonathan? Rowan widened his stance, hoping he would not fall. There, Jonathan's voice, instructing Silas the gravedigger, who had entered the room so lightly that Rowan needed his scent of loamy earth and decay mixed with ginger to realize his presence.

Their conversation over, Rowan stepped closer. "Mr. Kingsley. Why do the upstairs people not remember her name?"

That soft rustle of fine fabric. Was it a shrug? "Medical men. We are all body parts only to them."

"Not our Ursula!"

"Our?"

Rowan felt himself coloring. "Dieu, but that holier-than-thou surgeon's a fool, we are thinking, sir," he tried.

"We?"

"Her dog and myself. Did you not hear his growl? Keep that sawbones away from us, will you, Mr. Kingsley?"

"I will exert what influence I possess, Sergeant. For now, Silas has fetched your clothes from your quarters. Let's get some on, so the gravediggers don't haul your shrouded self out with poor Charlie."

Rowan's fingers grazed his open nightshirt's front. It was all the clothing he wore. He'd forgotten everything in his joy at sensing Ursula near so early in the day. Good God, and her brother had found them entwined?

"Ursula was early on the ward today," he tried.

A clipped snort. "So I gather. Here, then. Lean on me."

Rowan stepped into his Zouave uniform's wide, sky blue pantaloons, the tattered ones he fought in, not the smart red parade pair. Jonathan waited for him to tuck in his shirt, then helped with his vest. Rowan attempted buttoning the garment closed, but he could not find the strength, somehow.

Jonathan grabbed his arm. "I do not like the looks of you. Back to bed."

Don't fall. It would not do to bring them both down.

There, they arrived at his tucked away corner of the cellar. The cot welcomed him back. Rowan felt the sweat trickle down his neck. Exertion. Not fever, please God. Fever would finish him.

"Well! That is what you two were about."

"About?"

"She has not yet swept up your hair from the floor. I thought you appeared clipped, Sampson."

"Sampson?"

"Delilah's got you shorn, robbing your strength. And your glib tongue, apparently."

"Feels better, my head, shorn," Rowan defended Ursula's efforts. "Was the whistle playing has got me tired, that's the whole of it."

"I see. Rest then, while I clean up your fallen locks, so they do not fault her."

"Who would do such a thing as that, Mr. Kingsley? I'll knock the block off any that dares!"

Her brother laughed. "Eyes closed, Sergeant. Rest before the coming combat."

Rowan woke, his ears alerted to voices. A few dictating letters, some moaning, a card game to the east. The dog was gone, maybe off to the stairwell to wait for Ursula's return. Her lemon balm scent was absent, but the pine and brandy told him Jonathan was close by him still. They had better have it out. He sat up and planted his feet on the ground.

"Good morning," he tried.

"It is almost noon."

He pulled his hand through his hair. "Listen. Earlier, when you first arrived, how long—?"

"Long enough."

Jonathan Kingsley usually had many more words in him. He must be a man made terse by anger, Rowan thought.

"Sergeant Buckley, if you have compromised the virtue of my sister—"

"Surely she's seen more things in this place that might compromise her virtue than a man at his bath!"

"You were bathing?"

"Washing! Shaving!" Holy Mother, why did he sound so guilty?

Jonathan Kingsley grabbed his jaw, turned his head. "No evidence of blood. You did not cut yourself, requiring her assistance. Yet when I observed you both she was close enough to... Well, sir. Do you think me blind too? You tried to entice my sister, she who is innocence itself."

"I did no such thing! 'Twas she—"

"She, sir?"

"Aye, she who offered—"

"Offered what? Now what are you calling my sister?"

"An angel, a saint, nothing less! I think most highly of the lady!" Rowan heard his own indignant breathing. In, out.

"So, what are you yelling about?" Jonathan demanded, his tone suddenly light, affable. "Are you going to take her off my hands or shall I kill you? I will demand satisfaction."

"Satis—?"

"Humph. As our duel would put you at a decided disadvantage, I suppose you will have to marry her."

Rowan felt suddenly lightheaded. A fine sprinkle of stars came before his eyes, shattering the darkness with beauty. He reached out, but the stars wound around and sped off like a comet, leaving him bereft, holding his suddenly aching head between his hands.

He heard a burst of nervous laughter beside him. "Look here, you do not have to faint dead away at the thought."

A joke. It was some kind of Marylander joke he was at, then? His captain had no use for Marylanders, still in the Union, yet holding fast to their slaves, and half of them spies for the South, said he. "You ought not to make light," Rowan chastised this one. "I am not without feelings. Neither is your sister."

A snort. "What about my feelings? Do you know how long I have struggled for an answer to her predicament?"

Rowan raised his head, smelling the truth, at long last. "What is her predicament?"

"Well, she— well, the fact is, she would offer you no dowry!"

"Dowry? Are you daft? I have no sight!"

"Imperfections that cancel each other out, to my way of thinking. Do you not like her, Sergeant?"

"I would give what is left of my diminished life for her, but that is off the purpose of—"

"Diminished life, is it now? Self-pity does not become you, not at all. Is that why you have not allowed us to write to your people? Selfish of you, especially since you are going to make a full recovery, providing we can keep you safe here among the dying and away from the doctors."

"Oh? Are the medical men aware of your scheme?"

"Of course not! How long would I last as a volunteer if they knew how deeply I despise them? Touchy idiots, mostly. I know one thing: the more the surgeons and physicians keep their filthy hands off a wound, the faster it heals. It is a damned good thing they have no idea how you survived your first night down here. They are too dumbfounded to do anything but allow us to look after you."

"Mr. Kingsley. Am I not going to die, then?"

"Are the headaches becoming less frequent?"

"Yes."

"And your strength returns?"

"Yes."

"Well, of what else does recovery consist?"

"Return. Of faculties."

Rowan thought of the starburst. He would be willing to endure a good deal of pain to see another one of those. Did he dare hope for more than blinded survival of a few weeks or months?

"Come on, brother." Jonathan grabbed his arm and yanked him to his feet. "Time for a walk. Perhaps the air will clear your muddled head."

The brisk autumn day only filled Rowan with more questions. He inhaled intense, ripe scents. They were walking through an orchard, then? The fruit was not what he knew: not apples, or pears. It was elusive, like his sight, out of reach. Beside him, Jonathan Kingsley was quiet for once.

"What kind of trees are around us?" Rowan asked.

"We walked through rows of cherry and quince. And we are now among the peach."

Peach? Rowan felt his mouth water at the thought. He'd heard of peaches. What did one taste like? "Are there any still in season?"

"No. The last of them are already hauled in to distill preserves and medicinal concoctions."

"Oh."

Jonathan stopped. "You are disappointed you missed a taste of fresh peach?" He gave out a curt laugh. "Well, something disappoints our peerless sergeant at last!"

Rowan did not realize he was viewed as such a paragon.

"Listen, my friend," Jonathan said, "I can provide a substitute. Helping us to end this cruel war certainly deserves a taste of peach preserves, or, better yet, peach-flavored brandy, yes? Shall I endeavor to locate a bottle?"

"Do you make the peach brandy then? Do you live here?"

"God, no!"

"But Ursula does? She lives here without you?"

"Not by my choice!"

"Is that part of her predicament?"

"Enough questions! I have missed the morning coffee thanks to you! And I can only get blasted chicory root mud at home!"

Yes, Rowan thought. Stop annoying the man.

"I will remain here until you fetch me. Go and have your coffee."

Jonathan took his arm and eased him down in the grass. "I shall visit the storerooms, charm Michaelita who is in charge of them, then deliver one of her bottles of brandy under your pillow. I will then have my coffee, and return. Do not move. If you hurt yourself Ursula will have my head."

"Still as the sphinx," Rowan promised.

Jonathan's sprightly step diminished. Rowan heard him exchanging pleasantries, making a woman laugh. Was she Michaelita of the peach brandy? Who was she to Ursula? And why was this kind man always leaving things about his sister unsaid?

Chapter 4

Rowan leaned back in the grass. Softer than the creek side grasses on the Maries' farm. And clipped short, like a carpet, although not fresh-mown. The scent of fresh-mown grass used to make him sick, because he remembered his family's desperate boiling of it, drinking of it, in Ireland. The Maries were so patient with him, over his first summers with them, feeding him spoonfuls of maple syrup or honey to ease the great heavings of his gut at the smell of fresh grass.

Enough of that past time. The now had its own troubles. But it also had Ursula. He went over what he knew: Ursula Kingsley lived in the border state of Maryland, here, apart from her brother. Why? And what was this place that was large enough to become a hospital? She was a skilled nursing woman. She assisted at surgery and quietly did the doctors' bidding.

Quietly. That was different from other field nurses. They were good souls, but he'd never met a one who was not old, hatchet-faced and opinionated. Loudly so. Ursula glided about like a swan. Perhaps the rest of her was in opposition to those ladies he had already encountered too?

He frowned. And why should Ursula be young and beautiful? To please him, so deserving, the great prize he was– a scarred, head-shot, blind soldier with a small gift of tunes and causing her laughter?

Jonathan had made it sound so important, the fact that he had made Ursula laugh. Was she not happy, here in this country, the one he so admired, the one that marked the pursuit of happiness right within its sacred documents?

Now Rowan was annoying even himself with questions. He was no great scholar, but he was sure of a few things. That the sound of Ursula Kingsley's voice made him giddy, for one. When she'd touched her damp cloth to his chin, another part of him went too strong, too brazen. He had wanted to pull her onto his lap and kiss her breathless, then.

Yes, he decided. It little mattered what her predicament was. If she were full forty-five and toothless, he would love her. Not with the love he'd thought he had for Clotilde Brosseau before she ran off with the foreman at the lumber mill, or the Widow Caron who bid him a sweet farewell before she returned to Montreal and her life on the stage. This was not a boy's love, which was more like pride: in women finding him pleasing, in his ability to capture their interest, then gain entrance to their secret places for mutual pleasure. What he felt for Ursula was deep, abiding. Necessary to what life he had left. And likely as doomed as the other two, here in wartime.

He raised his head at the sound of light, shuffling movement on the gravel path. "Good afternoon, Silas," Rowan called out to the quiet gravedigger whose scent he'd come to know.

"And a good afternoon to you, sergeant sir. I took liberty to bring along another this day," Silas announced.

Rowan caught whiffs of cigars, soap, raspberry jam, and whiskey. Silas Keene's companion had been around supply stores, the expensive supplies that the officers bought.

"Bless my soul, Mister Rowan, if it's not you truly!" a long-familiar voice sounded.

"Aaron?" Rowan whispered, struggling to his feet. "Aaron Price?"

"The very same! And lettin' nobody call you dead and washed down that creek, no, sir! Not 'til I felt the loss of you in my heart!"

"What?" Silas proclaimed. "Our sergeant is your neighbor from the northland? The one you be seeking out?"

"He is."

"But he be a white man! Would of found him sooner if'n you said he was white! I been lookin' all over the grave diggings and through that crazy Louisiana guard regiment's servants! You far north folk sure peculiar!"

"Not peculiar. We are free. And some even have us some good white neighbors."

"Suit yourself. I got duties. You have a nice visit, then," he said, taking Rowan's hand in his work-hardened one, and linking it to his neighbor's shoulder before he left.

Rowan gave himself the pleasure of a quick, rough embrace with his friend. He had never gotten Aaron Price to drop the "misters," or "sirs," though there was a scant two years between their ages, and they had known each other since their boyhoods. That was on command of Hetty Lee, Aaron's small but formidable mother, who insisted on her son showing signs of respect. Or, perhaps, the Maries had explained to Rowan, a safe distance from all white people.

Aaron stepped back so fast that Rowan lost his balance, stumbled. He felt a steadying hold at his arm.

He heard no pity in his neighbor's usual jovial tone. "Captain Merritt, he sent off his sorry-you-are-dead letter to your folk. But he got me switched to grave and hospital duty, too, when I pestered him long enough, so's I can search you out and learn the truth of it," Aaron said. "Now yesterday, when those workers in the field of the dead told me the story of hearing fine whistle-playing easing soldiers out of life here in this place, I figured I'd best see if you found your way here."

"How do you fare, Aaron?" Rowan asked his friend. "And your family? And our Company D?"

"Last letter said my gals, big and little, are keepin' themselves well, along with our good neighbors your womenfolk, thank you, sir. Now, I cannot say the same of Company D, no, sir."

"How many losses, at the bridge?"

"Of that bunch, none but you, sir."

"None?"

"Oh, except for Corporal Bond, who we thought lost, but he just got himself buried for a time under a calvary man's dead horse. Your men to a one said you took everything from that cannon fire for them. A good story, honoring you."

"A fable," Rowan declared, frowning. "Bringing sense to this madness."

"Still, you were out front, as is your way, so you must let them have their story. Now the rest of Company D, the one got sent through the cornfield? We lost eleven outright: Carpenter, Bellows, Higgins, Greene, Murphy, Donovan, Cobb, Moss, Plank, Steen and Fowler."

"Decriss! Did they not observe wide formation?"

"Captain says they did, sir. But they could not drop and fire, on account of the corn being so high, you see? They went down like someone took a scythe to them. Twenty-three more wounded. They are scattered all over the hospital stations. Captain's been generous with his own funds and I been working my wiles to trade with the sutlers to get them some luxuries beyond sustenance to help them along. Only you ended up here, at this grand farm. The still battle-fit of us are camped at Boonsboro, not far. Captain Merritt's been surlier than a treed panther! He will welcome the news of your survival!"

"Not survival, Aaron. I am blinded."

"I know, sir."

Of course, he did. Oppressed people, like his and Aaron Price's, were good observers. Out with the rest of it. "And I am not expected to live."

"What's this? Who says such a thing? The saw bone surgeons? Paugh!" Aaron Price's jaunty voice softened as he laid his hand on Rowan's forearm. "Best get busy in your finest hand to paper. Or, well, ask one of the mercy sisters here to do it for you. Wouldn't want those women of yours stitching up mourning garments for themselves without cause. They plenty thrifty, your ladies! You will sure to hear about that waste till doomsday!"

Rowan smiled. This was what he needed, not to think of the Maries as grieving, but annoyed. That might help lead him out of this other darkness, the one surrounding the notion of his uselessness to them. It was a darkness leeching into his soul.

Chapter 5

Rowan dreamed of lending his warmth to that place beneath his mother's heart. Of wanting to be warmer, stronger, bigger, anything to keep her alive.

"Rowan shona! My merry boy!" her voice with its beautiful, lilting notes, called.

He woke, breathing hard. All was dark. Was it day or night? He listened. So quiet. Still night, then? Without Private Gray and his torturous breathing, it was even more quiet on the death ward.

Rowan lifted the edge of the featherbed mattress and found where Jonathan had stashed his gift, the bottle of peach brandy. He twisted off the cork. He'd never indulged in anything stronger than the Maries' hard apple cider, not even in New York City, where all manner of strong spirits could be had on any corner.

A single swallow only, to taste the peaches. The drink landed in his stomach with a fire that spread to his fingers, toes, and out the roots of his hair. He gasped. The lighter sweetness finally came on his third breath. Was that the taste of peaches?

Why his mother's call in the dream? It served no purpose. He had to have purpose. And she had taught him that dreams were powerful, and held messages of the dead, of the angels. Rowan made himself search for meaning, to honor his mother.

But thoughts of his future mocked his efforts. Tomorrow Aaron Price would bring his captain to see who he was now: Company D's blind sergeant, of no more use to them.

The cellar air became too close, too confining. Rowan needed the stars, the trees. He could find them now, on his own, without being on Jonathan or Ursula's arm, he was sure. He remembered the way, with the senses he still had left to him.

He took a fortifying sip of the brandy. Yes. That was better, that was the key to Jonathan's gift. Sips, not swallows. He tucked the bottle under one arm and felt his way along the stone wall until he reached the stairs.

Heavy doors, he realized, as he opened them himself for the first time. Back at home, only the church doors of Montreal were this heavy. What did Aaron call this place? A grand farm.

Outside, the air was free of medicines and harsh soap, the night alive with the Southland Fall– of harvested corn and ripening squash and beans to come. He knew the way, from his walks with Jonathan. He would find the trees, sit beneath them, and imagine the stars.

Another sip would sharpen his mind, keep him steady. He swallowed. That sweetness, at the end. Was that the fruit? Was he getting his first taste of peaches? Best try another sip, to be sure.

There. The rustle of leaves on the night wind. The orchard. Perhaps an owl sifting through, on the hunt? He imagined the trees standing like sentries, one after the other. He reached out, found one. Bark like a birch. Was this a row of peach? He held the bottle up like a divining rod. "Find your home," he commanded.

Why couldn't Jonathan Kingsley be more exact about which tree bore which fruit? Because Jonathan was spoiled with his own gifts: his wealth, his sight, his sister. So rich that he gave her away to the blind soldier who made her laugh.

No, that was a joke. Or perhaps only thoughtless, as the rich often were toward those considered their inferiors. Rowan had known plenty of that, on two continents.

He tasted the brandy again. Enjoyed the sharpness at the back of his mouth, and up into his sinuses. He should give his battered head a rest, for once, and not be so bothered about all the things that remained beyond his understanding.

He slid to the ground. Still warm, from the recent hot days. But sleep would not come. The Maries had begged him not to go south, said it was not his fight. But he'd wanted to see that land so tantalizing, so close, wanted to feel the air of that country which had fought mighty Britain and won. He would help them in their own righteous struggle to free the people in Mrs. Stowe's book, Eliza and Tom, people like his neighbors the Lees. Rowan remembered the night he turned twelve, smuggling Aaron's family across the St. Lawrence River, under the trade pumpkins on his boat. It was his favorite birthday still.

He revisited the excitement of helping his new neighbors to guide others into the Northland. Learning their songs, their stories, their rhythms on his whistle, learning his own English and Quebecois better, through teaching the fugitives to read and write.

The Maries could not understand how he and Aaron had wanted to join up with the Union army. Why? Because the women were descended from the French, maybe, a prouder people, a less beaten-down people than his own, than Aaron Price's, who were not even allowed to be soldiers, so they fetched luxuries for rich officers, and cooked and cleaned and buried the dead, in order to serve. There were no jobs for a blind soldier. Would the Americans now discharge him, send him home? What would the women do with him? Would he become what he never had been, even as a child: their burden?

He wanted to stay here, remain Rowan shona, the merry boy, making Ursula laugh, bringing the dying a tune to carry them over. It was good work, what he and Ursula and Jonathan and the dog did together. Was that what his dream meant? Was his mother happy, as when he used to make her laugh, even during the days of An Gorta Mor, the great hunger, when they had nothing to ease the pain gnawing at their insides, except his music?

Rowan drank to the great numbers of Irish dead, and then to his own, and then to the eleven new dead of

Company D. He imagined those soldiers joining him in his toast, because even with these bountiful trees for company, Rowan was suddenly afraid of being alone. That last night on Grosse Isle with his sister Talitha, who did not survive to the morning, now threatened to eat him alive.

A rush of broken branches. Something swooping in on the wind made his heart stop.

"Sergeant Buckley!"

Her fingers rode over his face, his neck, as if she were the one blind. And her voice, so different.

"Sula?" he called out, to be sure.

She dropped to her knees beside him. "Your bed was empty!"

"I thought to— "

"Empty! Gone! Gone from me!"

She was tracing his arms now, ignoring all the bandaging over the cuts and burns, ever so lightly it did not hurt. She smelled not of her usual starch and linen, but of fine cotton, and the night, and her fear.

"I went out for a walk, Ursula."

"A walk! A walk!" she squawked back, sounding like the bird he'd thought she was: a heron, coming in on the night wind. He heard her sniff the air around his mouth. "And you… you are drunk!"

"Maybe. A little," he realized as he said it. "Sula, listen— "

"No, you listen!" She held his head so close to her own he could taste her breath: vanilla and strong black tea and yes, there it was, at her neck, the lemon balm. "I thought— Oh, my dear, dear Sergeant, I thought—"

Rowan realized what the sight of his empty bed meant to her. That he was dead, his body gone with the gravediggers. "Oh, aye, then," he said quietly.

She tightened her grip on him. "Don't you dare! I cannot bear anymore! I cannot lose you!"

Her hands left him suddenly. He reached out, searching.

Her soft wail pierced the night air like a discordant tune. Stop. Please stop this. The wails from the coffin ship.

The cries rising above the fetid air of Grosse Isle. It was too familiar. He became that boy again. Do not leave me. Do not leave me alone.

There. Her long, strong fingers, slipping into his. He closed a firm grip over them, and drew her to his chest. "Anamchara, my heart, I am sorry to have troubled you so. It was not my intent."

She allowed him to hold her as she wept. Not the way she wept for their dead, almost silently. Now, out in the open air, deep in the night, she cried like a child, full of hiccoughs and sputtering. He leaned against the tree's trunk, feeling useful again.

And like a whole man. This was dangerous.

Chapter 6

When she quieted, Rowan planted a kiss at her forehead. He breathed into her hair. His fingers wove through it — unbound, blunt cut just past her chin, soft. He discovered the shape of her head-round, the feel of her cheekbones-high, under his thumbs.

She drew back, leaving him aching, bereft. And a little dazed from the potent combination of her and the brandy. But at least she was still speaking to him, in that new voice: nervous, high-pitched.

"I beg your pardon. This is so very foolish of me, Sergeant."

"Rowan, Sula. I am called Rowan."

"Rr-rowan?" her voice stuttered itself calm on his name.

"Yes, after a tree. The one you in America call mountain ash, bearing red berries at this time of year. In Irish stories it is a tree from the Land of Promise." He hardly recognized his own voice, slow, measured, careful. Why was he telling her these things? To continue the calmness the sound of his name had fostered, maybe. "My old hedgerow master, back in Ireland, he claimed the rowan's berries could restore youth to the aged."

Bloody fool, he thought, don't allow her to think whatever years between you matter! "And health to the sick," he hastened to add, too fast, slurring. What was the use? She knew he'd miscalculated the potency of the brandy. "Like your brother's peach concoction has done for me this night, maybe."

If she was still feeling shaken from her own attack of nerves, he should offer her a swallow. Where was the damned bottle? "My dear Ursula," he admitted, "I seem to have lost hold of that elixir."

He felt her weight shift. "Its remaining contents have spilled into the ground," she announced primly.

"Ah, then. Happy worms."

Her laugh escaped where those sobs had been, making his heart leap.

He reached for where he thought she was now, and found only air. Off balance, he landed in her lap, smiling like an idiot, he was sure. But she did not push him away. He even felt her legs shift, accommodating his always addled head. Worse now, with the drink.

Her legs, under a thin layer of nightclothes. No endless skirts and petticoats of the nursing women. A walker's legs, sturdy, strong. A new discovery, those legs. The sheer physical pleasure he derived from the feel of them startled him.

Where was her dog, her Friend? She needed her dog, now, to guard her. From him.

Her fingers glided across his scalp. She'd done this before, when she was caring for the wound. He did not know why she did it now, only prayed she would not stop. Talk. Talk before your hands start doing the talking.

"What is this place, full of chambers and gardens and good country air, Sula?"

The fingers stilled. "My home."

"Where do you sleep?"

"Above the medicinal garden."

"Your garden grows angelica, and spearmint and lemon balm?"

"Yes."

A hoot delayed his next question— was she mistress here? Was the gulf so wide between them? The flap of wings came close, making her gasp in surprise.

"Owl, was that, Sula?"

"Yes."

Enough with the questions she did not wish to answer. Stay in this glorious moment of owl flight and this woman's hands weaving through his scalp. Find out more about the here, the now. "Is the moon up over your garden, over us?"

"The soft slipper of a waxing quarter moon."

Her voice alone was now enough to ignite his veins. "Are the stars out around it?" he asked.

"Yes."

"Yours?"

"Mine?"

"Ursula Major."

"Ursa Major," she corrected.

"Close enough."

She laughed again. "I am a bear, then?"

"Yes, my great protector bear. But you used to be Callisto, the most beautiful of the nymphs, were you not?"

"How do you know that story?"

"From my schoolmaster."

"The hedgerow one, in Ireland?"

"Aye, in Ballinamore."

"Ballinamore," she repeated. "The name is musical, like you."

"He was wild for the Greeks, that schoolmaster, and made sure we learned that the stars of Ursa Major and Minor did not form a wagon, or a ladle, which is what they seemed to us poor farm scholars. Those stars held stories, from the Milesians, long ago Greeks. Where are they now, Sula? Callisto and her wee son?"

The fingers in his scalp shifted his head slowly skyward.

"Here," she breathed out at his ear.

The blood surged through him in response. "Ah. Now, where are the last two stars of Mother Bear's tail?"

She adjusted his head's position. "Here," she directed, "and, here."

Rowan calculated carefully and raised his arm in a line five times the distance. "Is that the North Star, then? The tip of the tail of her little bear? Polaris?"

"Yes, exactly. Polaris."

"Remember how I found Polaris tonight, blind and drunk, my Ursula. Know that you will never be lost to me."

He turned her hand, kissing deeply into its palm.

"Rowan," she whispered, a siren song invitation. "It's the brandy."

"'Tis no such thing," he protested, flicking his tongue out at the pulse spot of her wrist. He heard her sigh: long, deep, with a tiny catch at the end, a remnant of her weeping.

"Rowan, you must know things."

"Not tonight, my heart."

His tongue moved up her arm, feeling soft, sensing warm, tasting salty. He imagined her glowing in the slipper of moonlight, like a fairy. How he missed the moon, the stars.

"Rowan," she called his name again, soft, breathless. "I am not free."

"Of course you are free, you're an American." Did he have to explain that to the southern ones?

"You do not understand."

"Your predicament? That's true. Your brother is most mysterious. It does not matter. Only the gift of this night matters. You will never be anything but beautiful to me, my bear. Please. Let me show you how beautiful."

Chapter 7

Ursula was in new territory, led by this sightless man, a being more alive than she had ever been. She found herself transformed by his tongue's gentle probe of the pulse spots at her wrists, at her neck. The thin layers between them: his linsey woolsey, her cotton, peeled away slowly, artfully, for that tongue, always moist, always finding secret spots that made her breasts harden, made her core delight and fill with yearning.

His sweet musical murmurs broke the silence, as his fingers ventured along her thighs, then inside her, searching, finding, sending a cascade of her pleasure into the night air, heavy with silence and stars.

She fisted his glorious midnight curls to keep herself on the ground. But what he and the night air did to her senses ran counter to her efforts. That mouth, that tongue, those fingers were wild robbers of her sanity. Defeated, she soared, her scream silenced, stolen, by his mouth over hers. She collapsed there, within his arms, where he held her silently, his breathing ragged and full of … what?

Need. He needed something from her. Of course. What all men needed.

Now the cruelty would begin.

She opened her eyes, focused. He was above her, all in shadow. Beside his head and its soft glow of the swaddle bandaging, Polaris shone. She could do this, for him. She touched his chin.

"Rowan. Come inside me."

"I need not, love. It will pass."

"Come."

He kissed her mouth, then, delving past lips, teeth and tongue. She tasted brandy and peaches and the primal, driving urge that complemented her pulsing one, which was mounting again, higher this time.

"Chara. Have you lain with a man before?" he asked quietly at her ear.

She felt the silent tears spring, unbidden.

"Yes." She breathed out the word, and couldn't recover her breath without a sob.

"Not well."

"No, not well."

He launched her astride him. His hand cupped her startled face. "It may be better for you this way. If it is truly your desire."

"Oh? …Oh," she realized as he led her hand to where that part of him waited, staunch. She folded his long shirt back with her steady nurse's fingers, then investigated further. How smooth, even fragile his skin there was. It did not match what she wanted to do with it, where the wild yearning wanted her to place it, now that he'd placed her astride.

"Rowan." How she loved saying his name. The sound of it cleared her head, a head filled with questions about what they were doing. "Rowan, if I were to put myself, that is to say, descend upon … will that hurt you?"

His deep chuckle was not unkind. "No. We are not made to hurt each other, my darling," he said gently. "But 'tis you who need care, if this has pained you before."

"It will not be difficult," she said, hoping she sounded jaunty and brave.

"Not at all difficult. Not for you."

"I seem to be very moist. That should help."

"I'm sure."

"Still, might we kiss each other a little longer?"

"As long as you wish it."

"Sergeant, are you laughing at me?"

"No, my heart."

She approached him closer as the faint moon's light cast over his face. As the ugly, powder-burned scar disappeared beneath bandaging, she realized Rowan Buckley's face was a young one, closer to twenty than her approaching thirty. And there: a line, beside his beautiful mouth. A grimace. Suffering.

The poor man was suffering with his own yearning, she could see it now. Well, that would not stand. She covered his mouth with hers. He responded, hungry, with those wild explorations of his tongue. The juices within her increased their flow, calling for their joining. This is what her mother felt for her father.

She took that strong, patient part of her sergeant and put it at the center of her need, easing down. His hands traveled the sides of her legs under her chemise, cupped another practical part of her, where she sat, and in so doing transformed it into a place of charged beauty.

The deep murmurs again, more urgent now as he squeezed there, at her bottom, making her laugh. She eased down further and felt that latch she thought she had closed forever, open. A sound came out of him, a sound full of strength and power and pleasure. Her body had caused it, by taking in his, for they were now hipbones touching, one to the other, a womanman.

The fullness felt delicious. How could that be? It made her world, her carefully planned future fall apart, suddenly. Then his hands took a firm, caressing hold of her hips. He rocked her back, then forward. She took up the rhythm of those musical hands, then added a circle to their dance. This made him smile wider, breathe harder.

Beautiful teeth. White. Even.

She was pleasing him. The power of it made her feel as if she were rising with him, to touch the stars. She felt him deeper and deeper within her until, suddenly, with an exasperated burst, gone.

She called out, frantically, feeling foolish in her need.

He sat up, took her into his arms then, murmuring with a calming sweetness, then turned her to her side. From his new place behind her, his fingers rounded her breast, then slipped inside that place still pulsing, and began to explore inside her. Harder. Yes, harder..

There, yes. The stars danced, then burst inside her once more. She felt her back melting into his chest, losing all sense of herself in his protective hold.

"Better?" he whispered at her ear.

"Oh yes, thank you."

He kissed her earlobe. "You must not do that, Sula."

"Do what?"

"Thank me. I will become more insufferable than I already am. The truth of it is, well, it has been a long season without rain. I could have done much better by you this night."

"No," she contradicted him, like a willful child, not tolerating any view of what they had done but a perfect one.

"Yes," he maintained. "And it is my intention to work very hard at doing better in our future times like this one. You have given me a measureless privilege. Now, being what passes for an honorable man, I am compelled to ask you to consider marrying me."

Ursula's tongue grew thick. How could she explain?

But she soon realized that there would be no need to explain. Not tonight. For although every part of her felt alive and singing, Rowan Buckley, breathing softly against the hairs at the back of her neck, was now very far from the corpse she had first thought him to be. But he was sound asleep.

Chapter 8

Rowan was covered no longer by her soft, sweet, sparked-with-curiosity body, but with a soft blanket.

"Good God." Her brother's exasperated voice drove him fully awake.

"Do not kill me."

A snort. "I thought the brandy had already done that. Did you inhale the whole bottle?"

"Most of it spilled. I was not drunk. Not thoroughly," Rowan amended.

"How did you escape Ursula's notice?"

"I… did not."

"Oh? She could not move you, then?"

Rowan felt heat rising fiercely to his face.

"You are fortunate in that she left you a blanket," her brother continued. "And, yes, your peculiar trousers, too, folded neatly, here." He shoved them into Rowan's hands with a grunt. "Put them on. It appears my sister has more concern for your modesty than you do."

"Is it morning?" Rowan tried to change the subject as he sat up higher to don his pantaloons.

"Barely first light. Come on, let us get back inside before they give away your bed to someone with lice."

As Rowan leaned on Jonathan's offered arm, he heard a groan. Not her brother's voice. And Ursula's dog was not about. That left himself. And the effects of the brandy.

Breathe. Walk. One step, another. Now, speak. "Jonathan. I will marry your sister."

"Well." The man sounded pleased, when he should have been strangling the life from him. "Perhaps your drink-fueled night time excursion has done you some good. Seems like a family conference is in order. Bench is to your right, Sergeant. Sit.”

Rowan did. His stomach lurched, then settled. He caught Jonathan’s scent of linen suit and starched cotton underneath as the bench barely reacted to his additional weight. His sister was a slight woman, too, he knew that about her now. How much more he wanted to learn. Rowan faced her brother. “You were not making light with my affection when we spoke of the matter last?” he asked.

“God, no. I have been looking to get her off the shelf forever.”

Forever. Damn the man. What a way to bring up the delicate subject of Ursula’s age. “You are … her younger brother, I think?” Rowan ventured.

“Yes.”

“How old is she?”

“Does it matter?” snapped out of him, like a bugler’s call to arms. Anger, at last.

“No, no, not at all.” Rowan thought of the feel of her cheekbones under his thumbs, and her strong walker’s legs, He thought of the deep sorrow that seemed to live in her, which made the sound of her laughter a miracle. He thought of the feel of her in his arms and her wild rises to her own pleasure. He would work very hard to be worthy of her gifts. “We’ll suit.”

Jonathan let out a blast of laughter. “Suit? No one suits my sister. You have a ways to go to convince her of our plot.”

“Tell me. Tell me all I need to know. Why has she remained unwed?”

Silence. From a man rarely silent. And then a different pitch, deeper. “As her only living relative, it is I who should be asking you questions, I believe.”

“Of course. I beg your pardon.”

“Well, then,” the new voice continued. “What is your own age, Sergeant Buckley?”

“Twenty-three.”

"Twenty-three," Jonathan Kingsley repeated. "I suppose that is acceptable. And your religious faith?"

"Catholic. Roman Catholic. I had assumed that here in Maryland she is also?"

Was there another incompatibility, Rowan wondered as he heard that odd, nasal snort from her brother. "Yes, Catholic. We are descended from the first family founders of this state, on our mother's side. She is deceased, our mother. Are your own parents living?"

"No."

"That's good. They can be quite a nuisance, parents."

"Mine were not," Rowan said quietly, not seeking to offend, but the remark could not stand without comment.

"Living siblings?" Jonathan plowed on.

"None."

"None? No relatives of any kind, Sergeant? Surely you were not forged, in your dashing uniform, from one of Vulcan's fires?"

"I have people. Three women."

"Women? Women who are not wives? Or expecting to be?"

"No!" Rowan protested heartily, then wondered if Ursula had as many years as the Maries, who were all old enough to have mothered him.

"Who are these women?"

"Sisters. Not my sisters by blood, but sisters to each other. A widow and two unmarried ladies. They took me in, you see, when I was a child."

"Formally? You bear their name?"

"No. I have kept my own name. They thought it right, in my circumstances."

"Which were?"

"Desperate, sir, but not by way of the fault of the people who bore me. The women are my family. They will be Ursula's as well, if she will have me."

"Well," Jonathan conceded, "alliances are always welcome. And what was the nature of your upbringing with these generous women? Were you farm, town or city-bred?"

"Farm."

"There are farms left in New York?"

"I have seen many, on my way down the Hudson to join my unit."

"On your way? You are not as the rest of your company, your regiment? Not a New Yorker?"

"I was born in Ireland, sir. And raised near Lacolle, Quebec, south of Montreal, since childhood."

"Quebec? Montreal? In Canada?"

"Aye, Canada."

"Sergeant Buckley, you are not an American?"

"I am not a citizen of the United States. But the Canadians are American people, too."

Silence. Then a deep breath was inhaled before Jonathan Kingsley spoke again. "What in the name of heaven are you doing in this war?"

"I volunteered. To fight for the sake of a cause I believe just."

"What cause?"

"Why, emancipation, of course."

"An abolitionist. I'm giving my sister away to a damned abolitionist. Emancipation is not what this war is about!"

It was Rowan's turn to be silent, to consider this Southerner's loyalties. "No?"

"Besides, Canada is British—the British North American colonies, and some say soon to be in league with the Confederacy."

"Not this Canadian."

"Yes, well. Of course. Obviously."

Why did Jonathan sound nervous, suddenly, with these shortest of sentences? And how was Rowan to ease the man's mind about his intentions toward Ursula? The future. Talk not about the war and the politics swirling like a hurricane about it. Talk about the possible future. Rowan's thoughts began to come in French, so he started an awkward translation. "My women there, on our farm in Quebec? They will look after Ursula, should I not survive the war."

To his astonishment, Jonathan laughed. "Oh, you will survive. For I'll not take her back."

Rowan thought of Talitha, her hand in his on the ship as their parents' shrouded bodies where slipped over the side. "Enough! You and Ursula are very fond of each other, as I was with my own sister."

"You had a sister, then? What happened to her?"

"She died on an island, in the St. Lawrence River, Grosse Isle."

"Dear God, the coffin ships. The infamous Grosse Isle. The cholera epidemic. You. Your sister. You were of the Irish Famine."

"An Gorta Mor was no famine, sir. No crops failed but the potato. We watched food being exported as we starved! We call it The Hunger. And yes, I am a survivor, the only one of my family. My sister and I were the last of us, and she was as dear to me as life, as you and Ursula are to each other. Why do you pretend otherwise?"

Her talkative brother was rendered completely speechless by his outburst. Had he ruined everything?

"Damnation," Jonathan finally said. "What are your Christian names, Sergeant Buckley?"

"One given name only. Rowan."

"My dear brother Rowan," Jonathan said quietly, "sometimes the world we are given must be faced with something other than your blunt courage."

"I do not understand you."

"And that is your great good fortune. But I am pleased to inform you that this conference upon the subject of your fitness to marry my sister has concluded. Shall we discuss a wedding date?"

"A date? But—"

Something on the wind assaulted Rowan's heavy head then. "Smoke," he said.

"The breakfast fires being started. Do not change the subject."

"No. Too much for cook fires. Burning."

"What are you talking about? Oh, good God."

And then Jonathan was gone, footfalls fading, fine linen scent replaced by acrid smoke, and screams. Rowan's world of darkness now taunted him, made him trapped, helpless, isolated. Ursula, in her room, above the herb garden full of her remedies. Sleeping. Too soundly, after the gifts of delight they had given each other. Too soundly to survive a fast-moving fire.

Chapter 9

Rowan heard the bark of the dog. What did Ursula call the animal? Friend. He pushed the name through his lips, and felt the dog approach, brush his legs. Short haired, not enough to hold onto. But Rowan found the loose collar he'd braided from worn rags. He had crafted something for her dog to please her, something beautiful, to make them belong to each other. It had pleased her. It had made her laugh and call her dog Fancy Friend.

Rowan pulled the cloth of his shirt forward, remembering where Ursula had strafed his chest with those fingers, had gripped the shirt as she mounted him, leaving her scent. He pressed his shirt to the dog's snout.

"Find her, Friend," he said.

He grabbed the dog's collar and sent a quick prayer to whatever saint might be listening, to keep Ursula safe. In return he offered something important. He made the promise while stumbling along with the dog toward the heat. He would sacrifice his heart's desire. Despite this impossible thing he had achieved, her brother's blessing, if she did not wish to spend her days with a sightless man, even one who loved her beyond measure, he would accept it, without question. In return for her life.

Bargains. He should know by now about bargains with a cruel master of fates. Better to rely on his Zouave training based on speed and efficiency. And staying low, out of shot lines, beneath rising smoke.

The dog, as reckless as he, ran faster. Rowan tripped, fell, feeling the tear through trousers and skin. Get up. Move. He must move faster. There, he was inside a building. Something caught his shoulder, a wall, slamming him hard enough for the white sparks to spray out from his habitual darkness. The dog yelped, choking, before Rowan lost his grip on the collar and went down. Harder, this time, on a stone floor. When he was sensible enough to pull in air, he choked on it. He blew out of his mouth and nose both. Blood. Flowing hard and fast. No matter. Where was the dog? There, licking his face. Good dog.

Get hold of the collar again, he commanded muddled senses. His fingers obeyed. Crawl. If he could not rise, crawl. He'd done it before. At Manassas, and Shiloh, and Antietem. Crawl on his forearms, still a strong part of him. Get to her.

"Go on," he implored the dog.

The dog whimpered.

"Further, Friend," Rowan encouraged him towards the intensifying heat. Rowan's fingers slipped from the collar to the dog's haunches, crouched low through the heat, against the smoke. Her Friend had a measureless courage. He would not leave him now, Rowan felt sure, not while there was hope of finding her. Together they found air there, low.

Ahead, a grey shadow appeared somewhere on the edges of Rowan's consciousness, amid the darkness, the suffocating heat. Skirts, he was sure of it.

Rowan followed the skirts up the lithe form to the trim waist, its apron strings tied three times around. As his sister wore her apron. He blinked his tearing, stinging right eye.

"Talitha?" he whispered the name of the long-dead one.

She turned, her dark curls bouncing, as in the days before the hunger robbed her hair of life. Not a complete turn, but a short, playful one, tempting him to chase her, the way he used to around bushes full of black currants back when they were children.

Not a complete turn, as if she knew the full sight of her would cause his heart to burst in longing. But enough for him to see the milk white cheek, serene, smiling, and her hand, beaconing.

The dog slipped out of his grip, rose, and walked to her. Rowan saw the animal for the first time. Friend was a black dog with splotches of white and rust. A small dog, whose tail curled when his sister stroked his back. A clever dog, who recognized sheer goodness.

Talitha led the animal up a short flight of stairs. Rowan followed them, crawling, to a closed door. Friend pawed where it met the floor. Then darkness returned, like a curtain descending, placing Rowan back into its confines.

No matter.

Rowan pulled himself by his arms, reached out, felt wood. Cool. He found the metal latch, lifted. The door opened.

Friend whimpered. Rowan crawled toward the sound. And found Ursula's hand, leading to the rest of her, tucked into the narrow bed. He eased her to the ground. She remained still. He shook her, called her name, gulping in too much air, searing his lungs.

No response, but the feel of her faint breath against his cheek. He placed his ear to her breast, counted her heartbeats.

Alive. Enough. Get her out.

Rowan heard her dog keeping pace ahead, barking him forward, down the stairs, toward the air, growing richer, more breathable, until he felt the stone path give way to grass, blessed, cool, grass. And then the voices.

"You can release her now, Sergeant."

"Her brother—"

"I am here, Sergeant Buckley. Let her go," Jonathan said softly. No other words, no curlicues of expression out of him.

"She is breathing. I felt her breathing."

"Yes. Let us tend to her now."

Once they pried open his fingers from her nightclothes, he heard her cough, gulp the smoky air.

Yes, all right, then. They would know what to do now.

The strength in his arms left suddenly. Pain returned, between his eyes. The movement of the muscles of his face intensified the torment. What had he done to himself this time? Rowan felt something cold laid gently on his face. Behind it, he heard muffled voices.

"He found her. The head-shot, blind sergeant reached her, through that fury, when no one else could," they proclaimed, as if it were the end of some hearthside story.

Rowan wanted to protest from behind the cold cloth. It was the dog who found her. The dog, and his sister.

Chapter 10

The scent of vanilla. Then, a voice, talking softly, kindly, but from far away. Or perhaps he was whispering.

"You look terrible, brother."

Rowan could not move. Could he speak? "Jonathan?"

"Non other."

"And, Ursula?"

"She is recovering. Ease your mind on that account. But they are taking you away."

"Away?"

"Yes. You are too good for us, now, it seems. I had to sneak in here to see you, imagine! Who do they think they are, this army of yours? Was it us who left you for dead?"

"Ursula is not dead?"

"No! Good God, what have they put into you? Do they not know how much you survived without their concoctions?"

A sound. Glass bottle clinking against another. Too loud. Hurting his ears.

Then Jonathan's voice again. "Liquor morphiae sulphatis. Oh, the damn fools. Rowan!"

"What? Jonathan, is that you? Does Ursula live?"

"We have already had this conversation. Twice."

"We have?"

"Listen. Do you think you could write your name?"

"Write?"

"Yes! Write. Your. Name."

"Of course. Why?"

"To help her. You want to do that, do you not? I will assist. No need to even raise your head."

"I am glad of that. Don't know where my head is at present."

Jonathan laughed.

Then they performed their peculiar task together in the dense silence. Rowan felt the slender fingers close around his, he heard the scrape of the steel tipped pen. He listened carefully, and thought the paper heavy, official, like the one he signed when he joined up. He was intensely aware of the muscles he was using. It was wonderful, that intensity. Careful. Do it right. This is important.

Jonathan added to the silence, holding his breath, Rowan thought, until they completed the task. Then his words came out in a rush.

"All right then, done. You will not forget us, addle brain, will you?"

"Jonathan, where is Ursula? Does she live? What is going on?"

"You are, my dear brother. You are."

Chapter 11

Washington D.C., Walker House Hospital

The air changed, no longer the Maryland countryside, familiar like the farm at Lacolle: the hay and corn gathered into barns, the crisp apples, the sunflowers. Replacing it was the stench of canals and sewage and bustling bodies living too close to each other. A city. Rowan knew which one, he had trained there. Endless drilling, before the war started in earnest at Bull Run. This was the capitol city: Washington.

At first, he thought the hands bandaging his head were Ursula's, they were so gentle. There were even traces of lemon balm, though in its dry form, not the oil Ursula favored. But now the woman was leaving his side. Gather your wits, Rowan commanded himself, talk.

"Nurse? Sister?" he called softly.

He heard the woman stop, turn.

"Ursula? Ursula Kingsley? She's one of you, a nursing woman. Is she here? Is she well, after the fire, back in Maryland?"

He felt the gentle hand on his shoulder. "Shall I inquire after the lady, and report my findings to you, Sergeant?"

"Please, aye."

"If you promise to rest."

"You will come back?"

"Directly."

"I'll be awake. I'll be waiting."

She must have known he was bluffing, for whatever they had given him was already taking effect and sliding him back into thick black unconsciousness.

The next voices he heard were men's. The first belonged to a stranger. "There, you see? He is waking up."

The other belonged to his commanding officer. "And a good thing too! I was about to bring a bugler over to play in his ear."

"By all means. Make him deaf as well as blind."

"Sergeant Buckley!"

"Yes, sir, Captain, sir!" Rowan responded, instinctively reaching to salute.

"Oh, at your ease, you precious bane! I finally find you, at the moment you have made yourself indispensable to others! Most inconvenient, Sergeant!"

"Captain Merritt. Good of you to visit, sir."

"Yours is a strange way to show appreciation."

Rowan smiled at the sound of the precise, New York lawyer hard 'r's coming out of the man he'd followed into battle. He and his captain had got on well from the start, despite the man's scholarly bent and prickly nature. "We had given you up for dead. I wrote a heartfelt letter of condolence to your women!"

"Aaron Price informed me of that, sir. I would appreciate you not posting it."

"Too late! I am certain that they are renting out your room. You may never get back in their good graces. Now what do I hear? You have been stumbling about in a fiery conflagration, breaking your nose in the process!"

"Is that what hurts?"

"Fortunately for you, you have been spirited out of that Maryland death ward. You are being treated by the best physician in the army of these singularly disunited States and my Columbia University mate, Captain Ryder Cole."

The stranger's voice came out of the darkness now. "Stop barking at the poor man, Fred."

"Oh, he's used to it."

Rowan reached toward the voices. "Sirs? The woman, she promised—"

"Woman, Sergeant?"

"The nurse. The one who lately dressed my injury, sir."

Both men huffed before the physician spoke. "That would be my chief medical assistant."

"He thinks Tom is a female?" His captain clicked his tongue. "How much morphine did you put into him, Ryder?"

"Sergeant Buckley seems of a balanced mind to me. Fully sighted men have often times mistaken my aide-de-camp's beardless chin and gentle touch for that of a female. Tom!" he called out, "Please join us. It seems you have another suitor."

Rowan felt a little of Jonathan Kingsley's mistrust of doctors seep into him. How was this one going to care for him when he did not even know his aide was a woman? Suddenly the air was infused with a scent from home. Rowan's mouth watered, his stomach growled, as the two scholarly New Yorkers continued speaking above him.

"Tom, that concoction smells first rate!"

"How did you manage to find the maple flavoring?"

Corn bread. That was the scent, Rowan realized. Smelling of the way Marie Catherine made it. Hearty, rich and sweet-flavored. He knew it even though it hurt to draw in the scent. He imagined crisped crust, hanging over the edge of the skillet. And then, he saw a dim outline, through the lighter gauze bandaging over his right eye. Work-hardened hands. Female hands, holding blue-checked cloth around the iron skillet. He blinked once, twice. Was he dreaming? Rowan felt himself ambushed by his own tears, soaking the bandaging over his nose, blurring everything.

"I used the bounty of your mother's last package, Captain," the holder of the corn bread said. About what? The maple. That's what she was talking about. A donation sent from home, from a doting mother. Maple sugar, in the corn bread. Rowan did not want any of them seeing him like this, weeping. Only Ursula. Ursula would understand. Where was Ursula?

"I shall write to my mother directly for a replenishment," the other New Yorker, the doctor, answered, laughing. "Sergeant Buckley? Have you caught the scent? Bring it closer to our patient, Tom."

The one he called Tom did as he requested, too quickly, making Rowan dizzy, not being able to calculate how close the skillet was to him. And then he saw the blurred uniform of the medical corps through the thin gauze bandaging. With sergeant stripes, like his. The woman was a sergeant. She made a small, sympathetic sound before placing a steadying grip at Rowan's shoulder. His tears. She had seen the tears, and the mess they were making of her bandaging. Beyond them, the men kept talking to each other. Watch her, this one. She was clever. Clever enough to fool them all. She leaned in close.

"Are you in pain?" she whispered. About the tears.

He shook his head, embarrassed. "No, Miss."

The hand squeezed his shoulder. "Sergeant, did you not hear? You are mistaken. I am Tom. Tom B—"

"I will not tell them." Rowan sought to assure her, not inspire the fear spiraling out of her. Her fingers shook, lost their grip on her burden. Rowan reached out, catching the fry pan before it hit the floorboards.

That finally silenced the male chatter beyond them.

"Good God," Captain Merritt said. "How in blazes did you manage that?"

"Tom," the doctor summoned his sergeant assistant quietly. "My scissors, if you please. And bring the light closer. Thank you. Now turn the wick up."

Tom. He must remember to call her Tom, or Sergeant, Rowan thought. Captain Merritt had often called him what her captain called her, his aide-de-camp.

Slowly, the doctor unwound the bandaging. Pain made him wince. No. Sensitivity. It had been so long since he'd known light. Rowan squinted. The light grew brighter, the forms more distinct. The nurse's eyes were luminous, brave. It's to her he should speak first, Ryder decided.

"I beg your pardon, Sergeant," he said. "My over-healthy imagination found female hands in the dark."

She smiled her thanks.

"Dark?" the doctor asked pointedly. "Not so dark now, is it? Move the lamp, Tom. Kindly follow its light, Sergeant Buckley," he instructed.

Rowan concentrated on focusing as the lamp's flame came closer.

"Pupil dilating. Yes. Well, now. After the heroics in Maryland, your extraordinary sensory abilities are known far and wide, Sergeant. But only a sighted man has the reflexes to catch that frying pan."

Say it. Say it quietly, evenly, completely, and no more weeping in front of his captain and these strangers, he drilled himself, as if he was the most unsteady of his own recruits. "I believe I can see now, sir, though not the way I could before."

"As a projectile blew through your left socket, taking that eye with it, a full restoration would be out of my realm of knowledge."

He had no left eye? The thought hit Rowan like a gut shot. He was a monster, a cyclops. No wonder they were content to leave him with the dying.

Chapter 12

"You see? Not so bad," his captain's most hearty voice proclaimed uneasily. "And, well, the bruising, the face swelling will go down, will it not, Ryder?"

"Yes."

As rich and accomplished as they were, the two learned men did not have the power to change the image Rowan saw from the wooden-handled looking glass revealing his reflection. Sergeant Boyde's hands covered his, steadying the tremble that rode up his arm.

Ursula had lain with a monster. She had allowed him to take delight in her glorious body. Rowan wanted, desperately now, to look away from the swollen mass of bruising that was barely human.

"A small whiskey for our Sergeant if you would, Tom," the doctor requested.

The kind woman in uniform left Rowan's side, left him alone with the workings of his mind. He turned the hand mirror face down on the table stacked neatly with gauze, bottles and instruments.

Captain Cole wrapped the new bandage at an angle this time, to leave room for the sighted eye. Rowan longed to see the face that went with the lemon balm scent and Ursula's rich, beautiful voice, those caring hands.

"The bone fractures have caused the swelling. It will recede, I promise. Your blood loss was substantial, as in all head injuries, but there are no signs of infection at present. I see no facial nerve palsy. Do you feel any dead areas?"

"No, sir."

"Splendid."

"No hope, they told me!" his captain blustered. "That is, when I finally learned he was not among our battlefield dead! I had to pull strings to transfer him into your care. But now those strings are pulling him away from us when our company needs him most, Ryder. Damnation!"

"Sergeant Buckley was not hit by a minié ball, I suspect," his school friend explained calmly. "It would have shot out his brains, Fred. He would have been dead before he hit the ground. Perhaps a small firearm caused the damage."

"The wall. The stone of the wall was fractured by the cannon's blast, sir," Rowan tried to help.

Dr. Cole swooped down into his line of sight and smiled. "Ah, yes. Thank you, Sergeant. They never asked you, did they?"

The doctor's face blurred as he returned to the discussion with Captain Merritt. Rowan remembered telling Ursula about the bridge. She knew. Jonathan knew. But none of the doctors at the farm in Maryland ever seemed to be listening to either of them. Those doctors talked like the men above him were doing now, as if he were not there, only his damaged head with its shot out eye and broken nose, on a plate, like John the Baptist's. Still, Rowan listened, though his grief. It was a matter of survival, deep listening to people who had so much power. Rich people who did not have to be careful with their words. His family had the deep listening from generations past, because they were poor, because they were Irish. He listened, because he as the last of them.

"Now, here is what I suspect happened," the doctor told Captain Merritt, "the left eye socket's bruising may have caused inflammation that required time and care to lessen. How your sergeant got that kind of care in a damp cellar among the dying I will never know. But now that swelling is down, and limited sight has returned to the remaining eye."

"Why then, it is true what they say about you, Ryder," Captain Merritt proclaimed. "You are a miracle worker!"

"Ha! Merely a competent evaluation after consultation with the patient himself. And I am well trained."

"By two years of insufferable lectures by old men and plaster cast models at Columbia. I endured your endless complaints on every train ride back up the Hudson, remember?"

"Well, I was instructed in France after that."

"France!" Captain Merritt proclaimed. "School of too much fine wine and too many women! Did you attend a single lecture?"

"Why, of course I did."

"Then it was physician, heal thyself once the husband shot you in her boudoir."

"Why not inform the entire hospital of that tidbit?" the doctor sputtered in a furious whisper. He took hold of Rowan's shoulder. "If you have not lost all confidence in my care, let me assure you that, in short, your face looks worse than it is, Sergeant."

Rowan forced himself to smile. "I was not much to turn the ladies' heads to begin with, sir."

"We will keep watch and hope for only laudable pus. If you will promise no more bursting into burning buildings."

The nurse returned. She took a calm hold of Rowan's forearm. "Sergeant?" she called quietly, offering a crockery cup of whiskey. Rowan downed it in one swallow.

He then lifted his head until he found her. Dark, expressive eyes, short curling auburn hair, shoved back behind her ears. Rowan studied her expression, full of concern. But not pity. And not what he dreaded most, horror at the sight of him. It would be safe to tell her, he thought, this women in a medical corps uniform, with secrets of her own. "In Maryland," he said quietly. "They never said, about the eye, being missing."

She squeezed his arm and he felt an infusion of understanding.

Her superior, the Columbia and France trained physician, then came into full view. Dr. Cole was a dark-haired, impossibly handsome, clean-shaven man, Rowan saw clearly now. Young, probably not yet out of his twenties. The doctor's eyes were a striking shade of green, like spring leaves. He was struck by the beauty of the shade. Rowan did not remember such things as the color of a man's eyes leaving him breathless with wonder. He was awed by everything around him now, after being in the dark so long. It made him feel intensely alive. Would it last?

"Describe the nature of your vision at present, please, Sergeant."

Rowan took in a breath. He concentrated. "I don't have a proper sense of the near and far of things, sir. The lamp helps. The objects around its light are clear, but the rest of the room fades off."

"Interesting. Write this down, Tom," the doctor instructed his assistant.

"But sir, Sergeant Buckley must be tired, and hungry."

"Yes Ryder," Captain Merritt agreed, "My man needs—"

"To sing for his supper! This is an extraordinary opportunity! You do not mind a few questions, do you, Sergeant?"

He was a rich man, this officer friend of Captain Merritt, used to the lower ranks' service to his own pursuit of knowledge. But his eyes were kind.

Rowan nodded, though his head felt light and raw without its full bandaging. "I don't mind, sir, but thank you for asking."

"There, you see? This will not take long. Now, Sergeant, how wide is your range of clear sight at present?"

"To your shoulders, sir."

"And there is darkness beyond?"

"No. A blending, around the edges of things."

"Concentrate. Away from my face. To, say, the second button of my coat. Might you find—"

"R, C, M, with the C a bit larger."

"I beg your pardon?"

"Was that not what you were asking me, sir? To read the letters?"

The doctor sat back on his stool, throwing himself into shadows. Rowan hoped he was not to decipher anything from that distance. Captain Cole heaved a sigh. "Wick down that lamp and cut us all sections of your corn bread, Tom. Sergeant Buckley has earned his supper."

"What the devil is RCM?" Captain Merritt demanded of his fellow Columbia scholar.

"Evidence of my mother's indulgence. Part of the new uniform she sent down last month with my initials stamped into the buttons."

"Your buttons? He read initials off your coat buttons? How extraordinary."

"Indeed. Yet, think on this, my friend. Sergeant Buckley's restored sight has now ruined the scheme of your cohorts."

Captain Merritt frowned. "They are not my cohorts! And I would rather have my sergeant back at camp, turning farm boys and city toughs into soldiers. But he has been off, very inconveniently, making the legend of himself. Rivaling our first Zouave martyr Colonel Ellsworth, I should not wonder."

"Why should they not return him to you?"

"Exactly! And why have they placed him in the largest guest room of this house? And alone, for now? Ryder, I am outranked by these government scoundrels, who are in uniforms that have no trace of the dirt of the battlefield. And I suspect this new development. My sergeant's returned sight, even better suits their purpose. So long as he can pretend to be blind still."

Chapter 13

"Pretend to be blind?" Rowan echoed Captain Merritt's words.

He bit into a slice of corn bread that rivaled Marie Catherine's in taste, then looked for the doctor's Sergeant Tom to compliment her cooking skill. Stop. First think of the compassionate lass in union blue as: him. Rowan did not want the likes of that one to be put out of the army. But both Tom and the doctor were gone, disappeared beyond his limited sight lines.

"Yes, well, Sergeant," Captain Merritt began. Those hesitant words were always the beginnings of bad news from his commander. He also smiled in that crooked half-cocked way that meant he was passing down orders from above. "Try to think of it this way. Your duties here in Washington— this scheme of our superiors will keep you busy as your face becomes healed enough to be fitted for one of Dr. Cole's fancy glass eyes. You do not wish to be hounded by the blue devils of despair before your strength returns you to our company, do you?"

A new world of possibility opened up in Rowan's mind, driving the peculiar request aside.

His commanding officer smiled. "We sorely need you, Sergeant. After our losses at Antietam, we now have a half-dozen Pennsylvania coal miners from a depleted regiment being added to our ranks. Only you can drill this crew into proper soldiers."

"Company D might accept me back, sir?"

"Dr. Cole and I will conspire toward that end, yes. Presently, you are not healed enough to return to soldiering, of course, but our cause needs you in another way."

"What is this other way to serve, sir?"

"I have not been made privy to the exact nature of the assignment. But you may choose whether or not to participate in these designs of the government men from the War Office."

"Government men?"

"Until you are again fit for active duty, you see."

He did not see. But Rowan remained silent, rather than keep asking questions that demonstrated his ignorant confusion. He watched the young New York lawyer who had admired Zouave fighting men and their tactics while on his Grand Tour through France. He ran a hand through his flaxen hair, destroying the carefully combed side part. Another sign that Rowan knew. That he was now about to go against orders from his superiors.

"Sergeant Buckley, you have a choice, do not allow them to convince you otherwise."

"Choice? In the army, sir? That's what you might call a grand contradiction, eh?"

His Canadian inflection did not elicit the usual smile from his distressed captain.

"Not quite," Merritt explained. "The task you are being asked to accomplish, it is not strictly army. It will most likely go against your honest nature, if I know anything about this crew. But upon completion, they will allow your return to Company D. It is all I can promise for your service in their scheme, Rowan. A return home to us."

His captain knew his given name, of course, from his enlistment papers. But he'd never used it before. Home? How had Company D and its odd collection of overeducated captain and New York farmers and street fighters become his home? There was nothing regular army about this conversation. For the first time since Rowan joined up, doubt intruded.

He thought of Ursula. His sight was now restored, however imperfectly, and yet he would not even be able to pick her out in a crowded room. Yes, he could. He knew her scent, her hands. The smell of the blackberry honey she used to seal over wounds. He wanted to take her away from her endless toil among her dying countrymen. To his real home.

He'd build her a cabin next to the Maries, and lift her over a threshold strewn with flowers, past a kitchen warm with the scent of hot steaming clafouti aux pommes, and then into a bed's downy comfort waiting to help them make their children, laughing children who would never have to go to war.

From where were these filled-with-future thoughts coming? They were dangerous. He was a soldier. He had made a promise, he and Aaron Price, who had lost most of his family to slavery. Before coming down the Hudson they had vowed it together. To see this war through to its completion, or their own. They were going to join the same regiment, and look out for each other. Until the army had other ideas. Only Rowan became a soldier. Aaron Price was not permitted to. So he took what was offered. Aaron cooked their meals, found the dead, buried them. Because this country Rowan so admired, was a deeply imperfect one.

"Until you return to us, Sergeant, I'll bid you a good recovery," Captain Merritt said quietly, shaking Rowan's hand as if there were no gaps in class and background and countries between them.

Then he opened the door.

An officer with furtive eyes and side whiskers that stopped short of a full beard appeared.

"Major Goss, may I present our Sergeant Buckley," his commander said.

Rowan, turning his head to make up for his limited line of sight, saluted the officer.

"Yes. That will be all, Captain."

Captain Merritt's scowl deepened before he left them.

The major appeared slightly stooped and in perhaps his forties, a generation older than Rowan and his captain. He held his hands in a close grip behind his back as he walked an oblong trail around the room's confines. The well-appointed bed chamber, Rowan realized, putting his new sight on wider assignment. And he was lying in a proper bed with a high carved headboard. The room contained other dark, massive furniture and gas lamp sconces on two walls. Walls that still held shadows of picture frames. The ceiling was a good nine or ten feet in height, with plastered ornamentation of oak leaves and acorns around its corners. This had not always been a hospital, but it was being made so now, with furniture up against the walls and space being made for more patients, no doubt. Rowan caught the scent of cigars and whiskey. Was that from the room or from Major Goss? The man thrust himself suddenly into Rowan's sightline.

"Before you enlisted in your New York regiment you were a smuggler," he said, his voice marked rough by those cigars.

Rowan met the accusing gaze. "To what are you referring, sir?" he asked evenly.

"Slaves, belonging to my countrymen. Ferried across the St. Lawrence River."

Rowan heard an admonition inside his head. It had Aaron Price's voice. Don't feed the power he thinks he has over you. He smiled. "As slavery is illegal in my country, I doubt your charge would hold up in Canadian courts, sir."

The man looked momentarily startled. "You are parroting that scheming New York lawyer!"

Aaron, who kept his hard-won freedom in his asylum-granting country had been the one to enlighten him on Canadian law, not Captain Merritt. But he knew not to contradict the immoveable notions of his superior officers. Rowan's smile widened.

"Canada is under the dominion of the British Empire," Goss changed course suddenly. "Britain, a traditional enemy of my country."

"And my own, Major."

"Your own?

"The land of my birth, sir. Ireland."

The officer looked surprised. "That festering stink hole? Of course! How did I not hear it in your speech?"

Because I have been living among the Quebecois for much more of my life, was the plain explanation, but this man was not interested in his life. "Have you traveled to Ireland, then, sir?" Rowan asked back at him instead.

"Nothing could induce me there!" Goss proclaimed. "But Ireland is in the territorial span of the British," he blustered on, "despite piddling efforts of Fenians. Well. You had enough gumption to get out, at least."

Rowan remained silent, swallowing down his fisting anger. He had no desire to tell this ignorant man of the great hunger and how it decimated his family and his beautiful homeland and its centuries of rich history. So he waited, listening. He felt a blistering pressure behind his left eye. No, not his eye, but where his eye had been.

"In Canada, you have allied yourself with another losing people, have you not? A crew of lazy French farmers on the borderland?"

He did know Rowan's circumstances, then. Would there be no end to the insults hurled at people he loved? "I have not found them to be so," he said quietly.

"So… what?" Challenge.

Stay calm. "Lazy, sir."

"Well, Sergeant Citizen-of-the-World, to whom do your allegiances currently hold sway?"

Rowan unhinged his stiff jaw. "To the army of the United States of America, sir."

Suddenly, Major Goss smiled, revealing small, shining, predatory teeth. "Ah, of course. Your current paymaster."

"I am no mercenary."

"You will forgive me if I remain skeptical." It was a command, not a request. "You see, I wonder if you will be at all useful in rooting out this nest of Marylander snakes."

Calm, though his thoughts were on fire. "To whom do you refer now, sir?"

"To Jonathan Kingsley and his angel-of-mercy sister. I am told you formed an alliance with the two."

"They have come under suspicion?"

"Yes." Major Goss stepped closer and lowered is voice. "Of treason."

Chapter 14

"We believe they were procuring information about troop numbers, Union strongholds, plans, fortifications."

Rowan tried to calm his exploding thoughts, and the memory of the air of mystery that swirled around the two. "Rowan, you must know things," Ursula had said, before they'd become lovers.

Goss paced. "We were closing our net over them when that convenient fire destroyed the evidence we needed."

"Convenient? That fire almost cost Ursula her life."

"'Ursula,' is it?" Goss' ugly smile widened. "Ah, papists and your filthy habits! As I thought. Already captivated. You are not the right person for this duty."

Rowan faced the officer full on, daring him to shift his glance. Yes, he thought. Look at me. Already an ugly Black Irish monkey, and now a disfigured one. "What is the job, Major Goss?"

"To learn their information dispatching channels, and catch more of them. Our plan was to request the transfer of Ursula Kingsley and her benevolent brother here to Washington, along with every wounded Confederate officer who was in their care after Antietam. The Kingsleys might continue providing comfort to you, our hero, of course. You would have been bait. We'd make you an officer to honor your exploits, and place you here in an officers' ward— among the wounded of both sides. You are, after all, the medical corps' miracle, plucked from

Death's doorway. So deserving to receive care among your betters.

"The siblings might be less careful around you," he continued, "if they think you are still under their thrall, and believe you are sightless. Were you able to keep the illusion of your blindness, that is. But as your captain has protested, you are utterly without guile. That nature would not suit our needs."

Rowan didn't like the sound of any of this. And he didn't like the hollow tone of his own voice as he said "I accept the duty, sir."

Chapter 15

At first, Rowan heard only the sifting sound of skirts. Then came Ursula's scent, unmistakable, breaking through the carbolic acid, the iodine, the metallic scent of blood that never left hospitals, and would probably never leave this large room, this home. Now, all he needed to do was open the lid over his good eye to see her, at last. But although he'd stared down all manner of firearm, he couldn't muster the courage to take his first look at the woman he loved.

Duty, soldier. You are on duty. To find out if she's spying, to stand by as they hauled her to prison, if it is so. Did they shoot civilian spies, or hang them? Did they shoot women? Stop it. Remember to remain as blind.

He felt the pressure of the black patch that was now sparing his visitors the sight of the damage. He lifted the lid from the good right eye, now freed of its bandaging. Steady, do not follow any of the movements of furniture, cots, tables going on around him. Across the room. Black skirts, head bent. Men in uniform around her. She was tall. As tall as two of the three men who were conferring with her. How had he misjudged her size?

Ursula, his mind called out to her. Turn around.

She did. Her eyes lanced through him. Past fifty years, he judged, and with an expression that mixed disgust with distain, and, Good God, in the habit of a sister. Not Jonathan's sister. A sister. A nun. Like the ones traveling the streets of Montreal in twos and threes, black-cloaked, veils. Of what order? Daughters of Charity? No, those wore winged headdresses. Religieuses des Sacrés-Coeurs, with their flocks of children following behind? Others, from the more cloistered orders, heads down, brushing past him on market days? What did it matter, which order? They were sacred sisters. Nuns, whom the Maries had taught him to revere, respect.

And to never, ever, think of as women.

Rowan's mouth went dry. His throat closed. He needed water. But he did not dare make a sound. It would bring her closer. She watched his distress. Watched only. He groped, without looking at the marble topped table beside his bed. A water jar tumbled, fell to the floor.

Dr. Cole looked up from his papers, reached him, held a cup to his lips. "There you are, Sergeant, uh, Lieutenant," he said softly, then looked over his shoulder. "I should think you would demonstrate more Christian charity considering this man's service to your Maryland institution as it burned, madame."

The woman's face hardened further.

"I am not your madame, Dr. Cole!"

Relief flooded Rowan's being. He could not concentrate on her remaining words of chastisement, he could only feast on the blessed fact that this Medusa did not speak with Ursula's voice.

Ursula had been in the room, she had left her scent, that's all.

Dr. Cole's voice became slow and deliberate, for a New Yorker. "Well, both Mr. Kingsley and his sister are willing to continue to serve the transferred wounded. I should think that would free you to attend to your duties back at your motherhouse."

"Your thinking is flawed. We are a contemplative society. I am a highest order choir sister, dedicated to prayer and worship. But even the lower orders, who serve us, well, we do not allow a single sister to toil on her own, out in the world."

Single sister? Jonathan's sister? Was Ursula then, a scholar at the convent, with her concoctions, her medicine garden, and not a nun?

"We welcome you too, then, of course." Captain Cole's smile broadened before he continued. "Now, as you have no desire to serve men and no medical training, I believe our cooking staff is short-handed downstairs."

Medusa began to sputter at the suggestion. Dr. Cole was enjoying himself. He looked to the door way. "Ah, the Kingsleys have returned. He is awake! I believe a reunion is now in order with your patient."

Rowan stared straight ahead. Ursula was out of his limited line of sight, but the touch of her hand over his was instantly familiar, warm. Her brother placed his above it, as if they were again forming a three-way pact.

He turned his head and saw her skirts first. Yes, the stiff, black woolen folds, matching the other woman's. A nun. "Sergeant Buckley, I thank you for coming through the fire for me." Ursula's voice. It would be natural to turn more toward that sweet voice were he still sightless.

He did.

Looking past the square-bibbed collar, the full apron, finding the veil, a headdress, framing that face he'd touched through the darkness, in the night. Light brown eyes, gold from within. Sad, beautiful, wounded eyes.

And forbidden.

Holy Mary and all the saints forgive him, but he loved a woman who was already married to God.

"Oh, Sergeant Buckley," she whispered, "Your poor nose."

Deceiving her about his returned sight increased Rowan's misery. But hadn't she done worse? No. "I am not free," she'd warned him. He had not understood. And had been content in his willful ignorance.

Captain Cole's laughter sliced through the heavy silence between them. "Come now, Sister, do not fret! You and Mr. Kingsley are well acquainted with Lieutenant Buckley's prodigious healing abilities. Why, I think your specimen should have a care to not wind up in Mr. Barnum's display of scientific wonders."

"Or oddities," her brother's voice contributed. Rowan turned his head slowly, reminding himself to remain impassive.

Jonathan Kingsley was flawlessly groomed in butternut trousers and a blue waistcoat. A slight man, as Rowan had suspected. How had this Maryland gentleman found the strength to carry him off the battlefield? A gleaming silk cravat tied his blouse's high collar and was itself held with a diamond pin. His light hair tumbled off his brow in gleaming waves. In dress, Jonathan was the peacock to Ursula's wren. Did her hair, carefully hidden inside the white linen of her headdress, match her brother's?

Go away from there.

How had he thought himself in a league with this pair, Rowan wondered. He must seem to them what Jonathan had called him--an oddity. Whatever was going on among them was odd indeed. But could it be treason?

He should laugh, take part in the frivolity, the way he would have if still without sight. But he could not. He was failing miserably at his duty already. Ursula leaned forward, touched his brow.

"Are you in pain?"

"No," he said, figuring that would lose him that touch. But it did not.

"My," she observed, "Your eye looks quite brighter. Does it seem so to you, Jonathan? Doctor, might it mean—?"

"That I will have to change the color choice of the glass one to reflect more blue?" the doctor finished for her with an edge of nerves in his voice. "Indeed it might!" I shall have my Tom observe closer, he is better at judging the gradations of color than I am. Well, here's Tom now, with a small repast. Shall we allow Sister Ursula to be reacquainted with her patient, while we get our new staff members properly housed? Follow us Mr. Kingsley, Sister Philomena."

That was the heartless nun's name. Sister Philomena. She had receded into the background among them. Rowan must not allow that to happen again.

Once the others had gone, Rowan felt something he'd never felt before in Ursula's presence. Awkward.

"Will you join me?" he asked her quietly. "I'm sure there's plenty of food."

"There is. I will. Thank you."

He watched her hands lift the cover of the small tureen. Turkey soup. Root vegetables: carrots, potatoes. And something fresh. Celery. He knew them all without seeing, from the scent. His nose must be healing.

Her hands were strong, pale, beautiful. She put the first spoonful to her own mouth, touched it with her tongue. Too hot. She blew on it, as a mother would, before feeding a child. Had she done that for him in Maryland? She placed the spoon gently to his bottom lip. Her nearness did what it did, before he knew she belonged to God. He winced.

"Too much salt?" she asked.

"No. Are you having some yourself?"

"Yes," she lied, as she put a small wedge of cheese between two slices of brown bread. He would catch her now. He would catch all her lies, great and small.

"Rowan," she whispered, the name she only used in private, "They shaved that place, beneath your chin."

Speak, he commanded himself. Unleash that gift of the Irish ancestors. "'Tis Sergeant Tom's policy for wounded and their caregivers alike in this hospital: shaving daily and clipping head hair short. I've come up in the world, do you see? A model of good practices, this city hospital is. Sanitary Commission approved."

She did not laugh, or even smile. "It was such a small bit of beard. And I kept it clean for you."

"Yes. Well. All are not as lucky in care as I was with you."

Was. He'd never thought about them having a past. Only an endless present.

"I am most grateful to you, Rowan." She'd already thanked him, about the fire. Was she nervous too, then?

He tried to smile, as he would have, once.

"I was but hanging on to your dog. He led me to you."

Her breath caught. "That cannot be so."

"Why not?" he demanded. Too loudly. But who was she to doubt his word?

"That is to say," she amended quickly, "it is not what I was told."

And my sister, long dead, she was guiding me too, he longed to tell her, but did not. "Your dog," he said instead, "did you bring him here?"

"No," she said, bowing her head like a saint at prayer. "My dear Friend did not survive."

"No. Sula, no."

"Oh, my love." Her voice broke over the endearment. "They said they found him at the foot of my bed, where he always slept."

Rowan felt his heart thaw with the grief he felt for the animal. "I am sorry. Your Friend, he was a good dog."

"Yes. I miss him."

"And you? Any lingering effects of the smoke?"

"A small cough only."

"Have Dr. Cole listen to your lungs."

"There is no need."

"Please, Ursula. Promise me." Her name. Slipping out again. He felt the heat flush his face.

"Yes. Of course. If it would please you."

"It would."

"You know, do you not, Rowan? Dr. Cole, or his young sergeant, one of them told you, before Jonathan could convince or bribe them not to."

"Know what?" He hated himself, suddenly, for drawing it out, as he heard her take in another painful breath.

"Know why I attempted to discourage our intimacy. Know why I am not free, that I am not only Jonathan's sister, but a sister in the Church, with my vows made long ago, to—" A sob escaped her. "To—"

Her fingers were pressed to her mouth. She was weeping. He could not bear her weeping.

"To God," he finished for her. "Yes, I know. Please. Do not cry. Is Ursula not your name then, but your holy name?"

"It is my given name. I am not even a good enough sister to be granted a religious name."

"They don't know goodness, then. I am glad you are called by your woman's name."

"You must hate me."

"No."

"You are hardly able to stand my presence now."

"I cannot stand this!" He held out his arms, aching he realized, with the need to hold her. "Please, Sula."

She pushed the table between them aside and climbed onto the bed, tucking herself into the place beneath his heart. She fit there so well, under his chin, where he could monitor her shaking shoulders, breathe through the fabric of her starched headdress and into her hair, her scalp, a sacred place. Good God, what were they going to do?

Chapter 16

Silas Keene and Aaron Price stood behind his new superior officer, holding their worn hats in their hands, looking at the rug.

"I believe you already know these two negroes. They are now your accomplices," Major Goss pronounced before he left Rowan's chamber.

The sight of the men eased the pain that the past three visits from Major Goss caused in Rowan's gut. He returned the men's shy smiles.

Aaron stepped closer to his bed on a side winding path, then grinned. "Why, it be true then, Mister Rowan! You done traded a broke nose for your sight returned. Good trade, sir!"

"Never mind that," Rowan groused, trying to hide how happy he was to be in these men's company. "Was it you who told Major Goss of our… ferry service?"

"Sure did! Once I heard you was up for a new job. An advancement they say. I told them that you'd do well, what with the tales you could weave out of whole cloth when we got into a fix up North, on the river. Fine times, those were!"

Silas stepped up until he was shoulder to shoulder with his comrade. "You disremember something," he said in his slow drawl. These people, they took good care of Sergeant Buckley when every mother's son was waiting for him to die," he reminded Aaron Price softly.

Softly. The way Silas Keene did everything, Rowan was starting to realize. A smiling, shuffling black man. Most people took no notice of him. Aaron Price was the talker, the joker, as he had been since he and Rowan had shared boyhoods together. Now Aaron used his natural affability to procure a share of tongue-loosening indulgences-- cigars, writing papers, soap from the tradesmen to share with the wounded soldiers. Was Aaron Price a spy? Was Silas Keene one as well?

He had lessons galore to learn from both men, Rowan realized.

"Well, now is our sergeant's chance, don't you see?" Aaron told Silas, "to clear the good name of his lady and her brother. That right, Mister Rowan?"

Rowan was honored by their trust in his meager abilities. He had to warn them of the nature of their alliance. "Aaron, the small assistance I could offer you and your family in Canada—-"

Aaron Price's smile disappeared. "Small? Why, without you and the Marie ladies, I would not have my farm or my first seed corn. Our good neighbors kept us from being grabbed back and resold to the Southland once as well, Silas. Grave danger of that, on the borderland."

Silas shook his head slowly. "Cold but full of honorable, this Canada."

Rowan rubbed the aching place between his eyes. "Full of all kinds, as here, I think. My friends, the blighted way you are both seen? As shiftless and ignorant? Well, that is the way Major Goss views me as well."

"You? You be a Lieutenant in the Army of the Potomac, sir," Aaron Price argued.

"And, you a white gentleman, like himself," the gravedigger added.

"I am no gentleman in this officer's eyes. I am seen as a different race, the Celtic one, which puts me below human to him. You understand this, you understand it well. If we succeed, I'm thinking that he will take the credit. And if we fail. Well, I deeply suspect that we might be sacrificed to cover up his mistakes."

Rowan watched the two men exchange glances before Silas spoke. "I believe we three can prevail over that bossman," he said.

Rowan smiled slowly. At least he was facing this painful duty with the best of allies.

* * *

The Capitol city frightened Ursula, after all the years of near solitude. But she would have agreed to go anywhere to have Rowan Buckley's company returned to her.

He slept with his forearm resting over his brow, like a boy. Ursula resisted the urge to adjust his blankets, to have an excuse to touch him. They'd taken him away from the convent so quickly. She feared they'd lied to her and he'd died in the fire. Or that she'd dreamed it all-- his lovely whistle, the good work they'd done among the dying. And the way they'd loved each other.

No, she had not enough imagination for that night under the peach trees.

She heard Jonathan's quiet footfalls behind her. He leaned over and spoke at her ear.

"I do not like it. Why is he here? In an officers' ward, and being doted on by that New York physician and his assistant?"

She frowned. "He is an officer now. They have made him lieutenant."

"Why have they done that? When he can serve in no more battles?"

"They honor him. His courage. Why should we question it? Or question the care they have afforded?"

Her brother growled softly. "Our sergeant is blind, of no more use to them. They should discharge him, so we can take him home."

"He does not belong to us, Jonathan."

"He most certainly does!"

Rowan stirred. Ursula heard her brother's quick intake of breath.

"Does he know? About you?" Jonathan whispered.

"Yes."

"How did he take the news?"

"Better than I expected. He is such a good man, Jonathan."

Her brother pulled up a stool and sat behind her. She felt the familiar chin at her shoulder, and remembered that he used to do that when they were children. A harder thing to do now, with her headdress in his way, but he managed. "Sergeant—"

"Lieutenant," she corrected softy.

"Lieutenant Buckley is an orphan," he said at her ear. "And we will take him in at the Pines, will we not? So he's ours."

Ursula sighed. "He's a grown man, Jonathan."

"I have noticed that. So have you, sister. One who needs us. You, specifically. As a woman, Ursula. Listen, we had a good chat while you were recovering from the fire. Before they whisked him off. I thought it was the nuns suspecting there was something between you two, getting him away from us. Then the army men, they beseech your keepers to allow you to care for him here. Now why is that? What are these Washington devils up to?"

"What are you up to?"

His head shot up. "Blast! Your holier-than-thou Dragon Woman's on the floor. Hear her berating the poor scrub girl? She will spoil everything."

"Sister Philomena? How?"

"You know very well how. Eyes in the back of her head, that one. Why didn't they let another serving nun, like Michaelita, come?"

"Jonathan, you must stop this. I have renounced—"

"You were too young to know the meaning of the word!"

"I knew. And I made a choice."

"A choice you would not have faced if I were your elder brother. Well, it has taken forever, but I'm of age now. I will get you out."

She turned, took his face between her hands. "Jonathan, I am not in prison. I chose this life. You must think of the household at Fenwick Pines. I have put it under your care. Our people. You are their hope."

"No. You are."

Ursula saw something rare when he tried to slip away— his true face, without the veneer of cynicism. She took his hand, held it. "What do you mean?"

"Our Irishman. You belong with him, your good man, there."

"Jonathan. My vows."

"You were sent off too young."

"I knew what I was doing."

"You must consider another choice. You must consider it now. Well," he said more brightly, escaping her grasp, "I'd best be off to fetch more pillows. Our sergeant likes to sleep sitting up higher, does he not? These idiots do not even know that much!"

Ursula glanced down at Rowan Buckley, and allowed herself the full measure of the joy she took at the simple rise and fall of his chest. He was alive and he did not hate her. What was her brother scheming? How could she hope for more?

Rowan Buckley was a not a solution to their family's problem. Their dear lieutenant was a leap into the unknown, a sea change from the tranquil constants of her life. How she missed Sister Raphaela at times like these. Sister Raphaela had known her deeply, listened to her struggles, had given her purpose along with her skill with the plants. Ursula missed the older woman's gentle guidance.

Rowan's hand slid out from beneath the covers. It dangled at the side of the bed, looking like so many she'd tucked back inside shrouds.

Do not touch. Run. Your last chance.

The thoughts echoed in the hollow, frightened parts of her being. No more running, she told the thoughts, guided by Sister Raphaela's wisdom. "Perhaps you are not for this life," she'd said, without disappointment, without rancor. Ursula had prayed to change, to transform her life into obedience, contemplation, service to the holy sisters. She had already changed. She had changed by way of how a sightless man saw her. He had even forgiven her deception. She took Rowan's hand between hers, then kissed deep into its palm.

Chapter 17

The long opening strain of fiddle music pierced the silence. Within a heartbeat it slid from deep sorrow into a joyous dance tune. He knew the tune, Rowan realized. It was Apres de Ma Blonde. And only one person played it in that freewheeling style. He sat up higher, there, in the large common room, where Ursula had wheeled him in his mechanical chair.

"Jesus, Mary and Joseph," an expletive of his father's, slipped out of him.

The music stopped. He felt his heart had, too, until Ursula squeezed his hand. The door to the ward, which used to be the upstairs ballroom of this house, swung open.

A six-foot bird of prey in skirts filled the frame. "Where is your whistle, mon petit choux?" she demanded. "Why do you not answer my call? I wear out my bow arm in the searching of you!"

"Bonjour, la soeur chèr," Rowan surrendered.

The black-hawk eyes narrowed. She placed the ancient fiddle against her hip and drilled his shoulder with the tip of the bow. "Pourquois le francais? Do you think my English is no good? Introduce, if you please!"

He swallowed. "Marie Madeline, that is, Madame Picard, may I present Sister Ursula," he breathed out, finally releasing his grip on Ursula, and wondering if his life could get any more complicated.

Marie Madeline scowled. "It is the other way around! Always present someone in the holy orders to a lay person, foolish boy! Did my sisters and I teach you nothing?" She halted her fury long enough for a polite nod in Ursula's direction. "He has the knowledge of manners, Sister. Please see his failings in this area as his own."

Ursula returned the nod. "He has many virtues to make up for a lapse in etiquette, Madame."

"I am most glad to hear this. In his virtues, you may credit his upbringing."

"With pleasure. I am so happy to meet you."

Rowan's diminished peripheral vision caught Ursula's broad gleaming smile, full of wonder and interest and surprise. Marie Madeline's antics had accomplished that. He grinned in spite of his predicament.

The bow now tapped impatiently at his shoulder. "What is so amusing?" Madame Picard called him out. "Your captain writes to us of your death, then, from Aaron Price: no, you are not dead, for he has found you in hospital. But, comes a word from you? Nothing! Rien du tout! When you could have asked this kind sister to be your scribe! A few lines only, you could not accomplish?"

"I thought Aaron's letter would be enough, until I figured out how to say, to tell you…" Another person to lie to about his blindness. Would she ever forgive him? "What happened to me," he finished in a whisper.

"Well." A merciful softening entered her voice. She tucked the punishing bow under her arm. "It did not suffice, as good as our dear neighbor was to post it. Et bien. The two Maries remaining will keep the wolf from the door for the present. And you have me to hasten your recovery, for better or worse, thoughtless boy. This army of yours likes the sweet sisters like this one by your side, those who disappear behind their veils, yes? But it takes on nurses like me also, did you know? As long as we are old, ugly, and suffer no nonsense from pups."

"You are not ugly. Or old, Marie Madeline." He hated the way is voice sounded: too young, too in need of the Maries to never leave him the way all the others had.

"Again!" she voiced her frustration over his head to Ursula. "Again this one is contradicting his elder."

"But in a good, truthful way, I think, Madame," Ursula answered, that lilting laughter Rowan loved back in her voice. Now he could see as well as hear it.

He shook his head.

"So amusing to both, now?" Marie Madeline flared. "Perhaps my talents are wasted? I should trod the boards of the stage instead of my barns, eh?"

Oh, why hadn't soft-spoken Marie Agathe or Marie Catherine, the best cook of the three have come, if one of them had to? They had cast lots among them, maybe, and Marie Madeline had lost.

She drew in more air to fuel her bellows. "Out with your instrument!" she demanded, raising her fiddle to her shoulder. "No more patience do I have with you! We must bring joy to those who are waiting for our entertainment."

"Tout de suite la soeur cher."

"Dans l'anglais, s'il vous plait!" she reminded him.

"Right away, my dear sister," he obeyed her, translating. He groped, as he'd trained himself, for the Zouave jacket that hung over the mechanical chair's back, and found his penny whistle within.

* * *

As the sound of their music spread, Ursula watched the room fill with doctors, patients and nurses, all smiling. Only Sister Philomena, up from the kitchen, her full apron stained with stewed berries, stood, arms crossed, unsmiling as the sweet sounds reverberated off the ballroom's high, coffered ceiling. Those who could, danced-- with each other, with a coat stand, with even the most sour-faced of the nurses. But no one had grabbed her hands, rushed her onto the floorboards. Young men had, once. Ursula had not missed those times in an eternity.

She wondered if Rowan sensed the pleasure he and his great force of a French Canadian sister were generating. Of course he did. Even his curls danced against his nightshirt's collar as he played his instrument.

Ursula sat back, losing him a little more with each note. Let him go, she told herself. It is for the best. Why had he even looked at her in the first place? She smiled, examining her thought. Looked at her? He had never looked at her. Why did it now seem like he had?

Never mind. Soon he would begin to forget her and their brief, war-forged intimacy.

A one-armed soldier bowed awkwardly. "How can you keep from clapping, Sister?"

Once, she would have wanted to run and hide, even at this small acknowledgment of her existence. "I cannot!" she answered now, laughing, embracing the beat between her hands. She laughed, though she felt like weeping.

Do not weep. They might notice that.

The sly-eyed fiddler woman who had raised the man Ursula loved nodded in her direction before she slid her strings into another tune. Rowan's whistle caught it up. His playing urged Ursula's hands to keep time, becoming part of the festivities.

So this was one of his Maries, his French Canadian sisters: the oldest, the widowed one, the farmer. She'd traveled down from Quebec, clad in a fine wool gown of the deepest indigo blue. Beautiful intricacies of tatted white lace at her cuffs and neck were the garment's only decoration. Her dense black hair was salted with white streaks that only enhanced her beauty.

Rowan Buckley had a good life, surrounded by the love of Madame Picard and her sisters. They would take care of him once the army mustered him out. How had Jonathan entertained the thought that he belonged to her, to them? Rowan did not need them.

They must allow this woman who was music itself to take him home, quickly, before Ursula dissolved into her sorrow.

Chapter 18

Capitol Grounds, Washington

Washington seemed a grander, slower-paced city than New York, Rowan thought, even with the influx of soldiers and constant building along its radiating avenues.

The dark-glassed spectacles his doctor suggested he wear helped him enjoy his first outing away from the hospital. That and the walking stick that Jonathan provided, a fancy, brass-handled thing he used to tap the ground before him, reminding him to slow his pace. It also reminded him of his deception in the face of Jonathan's generosity. He hated this spying business.

Behind the smoke-colored lenses, he could take in wherever his diminished sight led. He and Ryder Cole walked together to the botanic garden site west of the Capitol Grounds.

"I believe this is the appointed location," Captain Cole said quietly, taking a firmer hold at Rowan's elbow. "Now, Sergeant, ah, Lieutenant, if you will sit on this bench behind you," he instructed loudly for the benefit of the scrutiny of passing strollers. "Yes, well done, sir," he approved as several couples turned the corner.

Rowan felt the sun on his face. He turned toward the healing warmth. Together they waited within sight of the glass structure that held living plants from around the world. His doctor remained standing. His leg shook slightly. He was a restless man, Rowan surmised. "This pretending that you are still sightless is unnatural," Dr. Cole muttered.

"We share that opinion, Captain."

"And we share a belief about the Union sentiments, or, at least the neutrality of Sister Ursula and Mr. Kingsley," the doctor assured him. "But they are Marylanders, a state of many divided loyalties, so we will endure this assignment together, will we not?"

"Yes, sir."

"This is the least I can do for a man whose recovery has enhanced my reputation."

Did Rowan detect a note of amusement behind the statement? They were a mismatched pair, Captain Cole, a rich man, by all accounts, standing guard in the somber, fine wool of his dress uniform, so different from Rowan's worn Zouave concoction. Marie Madeline's preliminary mending had succeeded in keeping him decent, but he was still arrayed in tattered sashes and braiding.

Captain Cole was supposed to be looking for their contacts from the War Department, but he seemed to be concentrating instead on the women strolling in pairs and threesomes among the park's trees. His interest made most of them notice him and smile, but he did not return those smiles.

Rumors at the hospital held that he kept a mistress, one he'd met at one of the many brothels that had taken over Pennsylvania Avenue's boarding houses since the war began. Maybe he was looking for her.

Two men in tall hats approached, one of them as a deliberate pace, the other darting, as if before enemy fire. That one reached them first. "Sorry we are late. It seems Lake here cannot tell the west from the south side of the Capitol building."

Captain Cole took a defensive stance. "I beg your pardon, gentlemen. Are you addressing us?"

"Oh, yes, quite correct," the one named Lake said. He cleared his throat and continued, as if reciting from the far end of a schoolroom. "Do you think we shall have an early winter?"

His furtive companion's thin lips compressed until they disappeared. "Frost. Early frost," he corrected.

Captain Cole shook his head. "Close enough to the code words. Shall we gather up Lieutenant Buckley and repair to that arbor, gentlemen?" he asked, before taking Rowan's arm.

Inside the confines of the stand of tulip poplars, Rowan finally faced the government men, dressed as the tradesmen Lake and Fisher.

"The sad fact of the matter is that the Secessionists are much better at spying than we are," Lake began.

"Besides, Washington is south of Mr. Mason and Mr. Dixon's line, a Southern city," Fisher continued. "The very confines of your present hospital are not safe, just as that Maryland nunnery was not. Even Captain Cole and his medical assistants all carry weapons, do you not Captain?"

The doctor gave a curt nod. "For our own defense against the snipers who we have encountered above the fields of the wounded."

"They may prove useful as we prepare to set the trap."

"Trap?"

"Do not get ahead of ourselves Mr. Fisher," Lake suggested politely. "Let us consult our notes."

Fisher nodded to his cohort.

Both men reached into their breast pockets for identical paper bound books. They began flipping through pencil-marked pages.

Captain Cole folded his arms and sighed. Rowan leaned on his walking stick.

Lake looked up from their joint study first. "Ah, yes. Our immediate mission is to make Lieutenant Buckley familiar in the use of a certain firearm."

Rowan frowned. "How am I to explain carrying a firearm if I am sightless, sir?"

"No need, as one of this firearm's properties is its own stealth. Mr. Fisher?"

Fisher reached into his coat pocket and displayed a weapon so small it fit into the palm of his hand.

"This is a .36 caliber Remington. You think it a child's toy, perhaps? Do not let its size deceive you. It is well made, a precision firearm, reliable and accurate. And it can discharge six times without reloading. Keep it at easy access, tucked in the inside right pocket of your jacket beside your famed musical instrument. Tuck it there now, sir, if you would be so kind."

Rowan obeyed as the two men smiled at each other.

"As I thought! Not so much as a bump, not the slightest indication that he is armed."

Fisher beamed. "Dr. Cole will accompany you to a firing gallery outside the city where you will kindly practice its feel and accuracy with your limited capabilities. There, then. Once Lieutenant Buckley is proficient, we will have added to the defense of your staff and patients, Captain Cole."

"Indeed. Well prepared for a siege," the captain agreed, casting a slow wink in Rowan's direction.

Fisher returned to their instructions. "You will leave your coat over the bedpost and mechanical chair with its concealed weapon at the ready— but as your ah, musical partner from your homeland has been repairing and replenishing it in her spared moments, best wait until it regains its former splendor."

Lake smiled. "A fine specimen of womankind, Madame Picard is, if you'll allow me to make the observation, sir. She approves of your regiment uniform's heroic Gallic design?"

Rowan exhaled. "That was about all she approved of my enlistment, sir."

"She stood against your enlistment?" Captain Cole asked. "Well, that makes Madame Picard's devotion to our medical service all that more commendable."

"Yes, sir," Rowan admitted.

"She had brought a wonderful lightness to our ward," the doctor continued. "You both have, with her forthright wit, and the music you accomplish together."

So, the doctor and his staff valued Marie Madeline despite her inconvenient arrival? That fact made Rowan feel better. But he saw suspicion on the faces of the government men.

"Madame Picard is a foreigner," Lake said. "Should we question her devotion to our cause?"

"No more than you need to question mine," Rowan said, his patience gone.

"Or mine," his doctor seconded. "My enlistment also met with family disapproval. Now, it grows late and my patient is tired. Kindly outline this plan of yours so we can be about the business of clearing Sister Ursula of these ridiculous suspicions."

Walker House, November 1862

Dusk was turning into night. One of their times. Or it used to be. Rowan caught sight of Ursula closing the book on the wounded Vermont sharpshooter's night table. As she rose and walked his way, he smiled, enjoying the familiar quiet sifting of her skirts. Then, a shadow passed between them.

"Rowan. I am here," Marie Madeline announced herself, as if she were Lafayette coming ashore to save America again.

Behind her, Ursula retreated into the room's shadows.

He frowned, remembering to steady his eye's stare ahead and not on her or her tray of remedies and comforts. "She is avoiding me."

Marie Madeline looked over her shoulder, catching the last of Ursula's skirts as they disappeared beyond the doorway. "Is she?"

"Because of you. Your hovering. Go plague someone stronger."

"You are plenty strong, petit choux."

"Then, someone weaker."

"You are making no sense, Rowan." She sat on the bed beside him and felt his forehead. "I think that you are in love, little brother," she said quietly. "A forbidden love, yes?"

Chapter 19

Rowan groaned, but was glad Marie Madeline had found him out so soon. Her expression did not change as she wrung out a lavender-scented cloth over his bedside table's basin and wiped his face.

He knew her tactics. She was not going to speak. She was waiting for him.

He drew in a shaking breath. "All the nurses are called 'sister,' you see?"

"I see more than you would like me to, I think."

"Yes, well. I should have known, but by the time I even had sense to suspect, I was hip deep in it."

She blotted the drops that clung to his face. "Not hip only, I think. She has your heart, the little sister." Marie Madeline let out a soft sigh. "And she?"

"She is blameless, and tried to warn me."

"But she was not saying why, in these warnings?"

"Not in so many words."

"Rowan, English is nothing if not a clear language, no? 'Sergeant Buckley, I am a nun, please do not treat me like a woman.' Would that not have put an end to it?"

"Of course! An end. If she had."

"Things were not so simple between you, then."

"Well, they are simple now."

"Perhaps, no." She sat forward in the chair, and planted her feet on the floorboards. "I came here to be of help, and then accompany you home, little brother."

"I cannot leave, Marie Madeline."

"Yes. This your superiors have made clear to me. And it is due to something more than being fitted for your beautiful glass eye. That may be done in Montreal, though perhaps not so well as by the handsome captain doctor, I will grant you. That one, he is well trained. In France, of course. Et Bien. Considérons maintenant la situation. You are connected, you and the shy sister, by more than your affection for each other, yes? In a way that is dangerous to you both?"

Rowan exhaled slowly.

"Yes," she answered for him. And waited. Slowly, Rowan turned his head toward the wall. Caught. He was miserable at this business. He saw Marie Madeline's shadow as she extinguished the wick of the lamp at his bedside.

"And this connection causes more sadness. I will not compound it, my darling," she whispered, stretching her long fingers through his scalp, fingers calloused at the tips from her fiddle playing.

That's how he knew her touch, even in the dark. Each of the Maries had such different hands. As a motherless child, he had felt her calluses the least. Marie Agathe and Marie Catherine were more generous with their affections back then. Not that any of the women of Chateau Picard coddled him. But he had grown up confident of his worth in their regard.

His eldest sister moved in closer, pressing her lips to his temple, a place now scarred and ugly. He felt a burn at the back of his throat, and tried to expel it in a breath, but released a sob instead.

"It hurts you?" she said, apology in her voice.

"Not there," he assured her.

She folded her mighty wingspan around him then, as she had a few times during that first year with them, when he had felt safe enough to weep for all his losses. Rowan gave himself over to his new grief, safe again under those wings.

Mrs. Bell's Tea Room, Washington

"I am of the French people and so, seldom wrong about matters of the heart, young man. My brother and your sister, they love each other."

Jonathan Kingsley grinned. He liked Rowan's no-nonsense sister. "I think you are quite correct, dear lady."

Their steaming tea tray arrived. Although the other patrons of the place only nodded at the servants, Madame Picard stood, took the tray from the white capped girl's hands and placed it on their table. "I will find you if we require anything more, my dear," she dismissed, with a pat of the girl's hands that produced a shy smile.

Then the formidable woman was back to business, pouring their tea, slipping an apple fritter onto his plate and before him. "So. Good. We are in agreement. The question then becomes what to do about this?"

"Convince her to leave the convent." Jonathan tried to make it sound easy.

"Oh? When you have failed in this?"

Caught. "Not for want of trying."

"And my brother, he also attempted?"

"No. Too honorable."

She sniffed. "I think, no." She took up the teacup between her hands, ignoring the delicate handle, and drank deeply. "Guilty, it may be, over his own feelings. Sightless or no, he is a man. And she, a woman, though in the tower of piety for years. How many years?"

"Tower?" Jonathan smiled slowly. "Of course, that's exactly what the convent has been. A tower. Since she was fourteen."

"Fourteen years? So young and yet so sure she wanted to take the veil?"

"Not sure at all. Forced."

"Decriss! By whom?"

"My father."

"A father does such a thing?"

"Her stepfather. We shared a mother."

"One who is now dead?"

"Yes, Madame."

"Inheritance, then."

"Yes, exactly. From her father, who died when she was very young. She does not even carry his name, but ours. I used to think it was a sign of love, for Ursula, for our mother, making us one family, with one name. Now I think, even then, he was scheming for control. Ursula is heir to an inheritance about which I know little, and, from our mother's estate, a plantation, of which I know far more than pleases me."

"And why is this?"

"I am its overseer, Madame. As decreed in our mother's will."

Jonathan tried drinking the tea the way Rowan's sister did, in straightforward swallows, not sips. It worked. He felt restored. "You catch onto things much faster than Lieutenant Buckley, Madame."

"Him! We keep him only to have his music."

"He makes my sister laugh. That is my excuse."

"A good enough one. There is too little laughter in this world, young man."

She sighed hard, signaling a progression in her interrogation, Jonathan thought. "Eh bien. We understand each other then. Eat more of your tart, though it needs less lard and more currants, I think. Do you sweeten everything with cane sugar here in this country? Where is the maple, the honey?"

"I—"

"You do not give a thought to what sustenance is put before you! City people!"

"I am country bred, Madame Picard!" he objected. "On Maryland's Eastern shore, where we have a very fine cook in our Miriam. She keeps bee skeps in her kitchen garden for their honey."

Madame Picard gifted him with a wide smile. "You must ask this fine woman for a traveling jar of the elixir. It will sustain you in this city of many maladies. And bring some to my brother and his lady as well, yes? Now. Tell me more of the little Sister's troubles."

Jonathan considered carefully, forcing himself to speak of dark family matters to this woman who was intent on whisking Rowan back up to that frozen Canadian place from which they had come. Might she become an ally? "That year when Ursula was fourteen and I seven, my father demanded she marry his cousin, a man twenty years her elder. We used to run and hide among the rocks on the shore when he visited, taking her up on his knee like a treasured child. She stood in the waves to blow away his scent of the drink. They thought they could coax her with promises of running her own household and grand parties, but Ursula, in the end, she refused to marry him."

"Brave girl!"

"Yes. Then something happened. Something terrible happened on the night of one of the parties."

"What is it that happened, my dear?"

"I don't know. But everything changed after that night. Our mother grew pale, sickly. She began to die that night, I think. Soon my sister left us."

Jonathan looked down at his half-eaten tart. "I listened to Mama's pleas, there, beyond my door. At first he told her to trust the sisters, that it would not be long, that Ursula would come to her senses and be returned to us. I suppose he thought the simple convent life, deprived of dancing masters and cream cakes, would make her beg to come back on his terms. We wrote to her, Mama and I, for years, although he would not tell us where she was—what convent, what motherhouse. But Ursula refused to answer any letters, so my father insisted."

Jonathan watched hands as worn as their Miriam's, but with lace folded back from the cuffs, fill his empty cup as he found the words to continue. "My sister did not bend to his will. But she was gone. Gone from us."

"Ma chouette," Madame Picard said softly, more softly than he thought she could speak. Jonathan did not know what the word meant, but took comfort from her tone. "How did you find her again?" she asked.

"Miriam's uncle, Alfred. He's our groomsman at Fenwick Pines. Along with Miriam, they manage the place fine, and that's the truth of it. Well, Alfred, he took pity on me at our mother's funeral. He slipped me a receipt. Of yearly payment for room and board at the convent. Alfred rescued it from the ashes of the fireplace.

"So I began visiting Ursula. She was so different. So quiet and sad. And grateful, imagine. Grateful to the nuns for doing his bidding all these years. She had her own quarters, more comfortable than nuns of the lower orders, the ones who wait on the queen sisters— the ones who read and sing the Divine Office the day long. After her schooling, she took her place among them, the domestics, who toil for the others. Her friend Sister Raphaela encouraged her knack for the plants, medicinals, and the healing. And learning. When Sister Raphaela was head woman, she allowed Ursula books, besides the prayer ones. She treated my sister like a scholar. Some said she was grooming Ursula to become a high office nun, and even take her own esteemed place at the convent. But Sister Raphaela died from injuries after a fall last year, and there was no more such talk. Ursula has a small estate from our mother, but she is her father's sole heir, Madame Picard. Her inheritance from him remains in trust with his solicitor until she marries."

"Marries? What of her vows?"

"I made that my job, you see? To find her a man for whom she will renounce her vows. If unmarried, the will keeps her from taking the final one, of poverty, until she reaches the age of thirty, you see? After which she can become fully theirs and decide that her inheritance will go to the church."

"And when is that to be? This birthday?"

"April, 1865. The church will have her and her fortune locked up tight then."

A stillness came over the widow as she folded her hands. Jonathan sensed the warmth of the tea room's fire gather around her. When she closed her eyes even the chatter of the patrons seemed to soften. She inhaled deeply and opened her eyes. "Have you told our Rowan these things, ma chouette?"

"Him?" He frowned. "I do have some concern for my sister's happiness, Madame. I must make sure he will stand by her before he knows he has got himself an heiress on his line."

Madame Picard shook her head, seeing through all his posturing, Jonathan was sure.

"What do you call me, Madame Picard?" he asked quietly. "What is a chouette??"

That remarkable face softened again. "My owl. For your wisdom, mon chéri. And what of you in all this?"

"Me?"

"Are you not risking your father's displeasure? And thereby your own inheritance?"

"I have no desire to add another feckless plantation owner to Maryland's troubles. And my father is something much worse. He is not a kind man, or master. His greed separated us from Ursula and drove my mother to her grave. Either Rowan Buckley or this war will bring him down at last. I would rather it be Sargent Buckley. The chances for our people will be better."

"Your people?"

"Miriam, Alfred, and a household of eighty-three souls at present. Slaves, Madame, I am very sorry to inform you. Families of which I am struggling to keep whole as my father goes on about his debt-ridden scheming."

"What scheming?"

"I suspect he might have worked out something with the church and the convent's new Mother Superior."

"Sister Philomena, of the imperial nature?"

"That very one. Or he may be looking for a more direct route."

"Yes?"

"To marry Ursula himself. Now that he's sold half his own people to cover his debts, and his credit is running low."

One of her dark brows quirked up. "Does your sister know of this possibility?"

He considered. "I have not told her this last concern, but I think, yes, she knows."

"And still she hesitates to acquire my sturdy Irish brother as a husband?"

"Believe it or not."

Madame Picard frowned. "I thought the injury was to his head, not hers!"

Jonathan wondered how many husbands the Widow Picard might have worn out. He laughed, thinking that perhaps they had not minded.

She changed course then. "My Rowan and your Ursula. Have they been alone, these two?"

"Alone? Indeed yes, every chance I could manage it. I caught them kissing once."

"And did you not exert your brother's rights then, and demand they wed?"

"Well, she might have been only shaving him. What if the razor had slipped?"

Those piercing eyes narrowed. "How is it said? Where there is smoke, there may be fire."

"You mean… Do you think so, Madame?"

"I think I know the look of lovers."

"Truly? Then it is a damned good thing that I already—"

"What? What have you done, Mr. Kingsley?"

"Jonathan!" his sister called from the teahouse doorway, saving him. She approached their table with the confident grace he remembered from their childhood. It was that grace that won the attention of a few patrons, even more than her nun's habit, he was sure. Or perhaps Washington city was growing accustomed to fine homes being turned into hospitals, full of wounded soldiers and their holy orders caregivers. Ursula smiled warmly. "You have met our dear Madame Picard, I see," she said.

He stood. "Met? She has already refused three of my offers of marriage."

His sister's cheeks dimpled. She had light brown curls on either side of those dimples, once, Jonathan remembered.

"Of course she refused!" Ursula laughed, taking his hand. "This lady is quite sensible. Come back to the hospital, both of you! Captain Cole has found us a piano, imagine!"

Chapter 20

Captain Cole and his medical assistants moved beds and furniture until a dance floor appeared in the middle of the ballroom. Ursula tried to quell the longing in her heart as she watched the small circle gather around the piano.

Jonathan sounded a note for Madame Picard's fiddle's tuning.

A prickling began in Ursula's fingers. She hadn't felt it for years, not since she longed to take over the convent's organ from Sister Adelina who played even the most joyous hymns like funeral dirges. Her request was refused, of course. That became the first of her many lessons in humility.

Never mind. Stay here, Ursula told herself, in this luminous present, with her brother, who had brought Rowan, his tin whistle and Madame Picard and her fiddle into her life. And now, a piano, returning, like a long-lost friend. Did someone continue to teach Jonathan to play after she'd left home? There was so much about her brother she had yet to learn.

Their audience was patient, eager, even the recent amputees who hadn't smiled for days. Such power the mere anticipation of Rowan's music had!

Her own playing used to lighten her mother's burdens, hadn't it? Or was thinking so another of her sins of pride?

"My sister will provide our accompaniment, of course!" Jonathan announced.

She shot him a warning glance.

"Come, you have heard this Irish devil's melodies long enough," he insisted. "See if you can find us some chords to go with them."

"Chords. Yes," Ursula heard herself say with much more courage than she felt. She made her feet walk toward their circle.

Jonathan pressed her down onto the piano stool, then led Rowan's hand to her shoulder. He took hold, leaning closer, the way he used to before the fire. Here, in this public place.

"It will be all right, Ursa Major," he whispered her secret name. "Just pound away and keep us grounded. She tends to raise roofs, does Marie Madeline, without a little grounding."

As if planned, his sister let out a stream of high-flying notes across her strings.

Ursula looked beside Rowan's patched eye socket into the remaining eye. She could have sworn she spied a glint of pleasure. Its effect was so powerful she wanted to take flight. It must be her heart's desire surely, not reality, this feeling that he could see her, and that the sight of her pleased him.

Her feeling did not stand up to any objective consideration. As his general health improved here in Washington City, Rowan seemed, if anything, less adept at using his other senses. In Maryland he had somehow fit seamlessly into his surroundings. Here he moved too quickly. Even using his walking stick, she had to steer him around furniture.

"What shall we play?" his formidable sister deferred to him.

He grinned, turning his head toward Madame Picard's voice. A careful, considered turn, not the instinctual way he used to turn toward voices. "'Après de ma blonde,' of course," he decided.

Ursula loved the lively, sparkling tune since she'd first heard Rowan capture its notes. Did he know that? But how was she to keep up with it at the piano?

"Key?" she made herself ask.

"Will D do for you, ma chère soeur?" Madame Picard asked as she swept her bow across the string. Then, lower, "As it is the only key that one's whistle can play."

Ursula nodded, unable to maintain her composure under the older woman's direct gaze. How splendid Madame Picard was. How had Rowan even take any notice her, when he was used to such women? "My dear sister" the woman called her, with such ease. Ursula wished that she and Madame Picard were true sisters.

Rowan's penny whistle rang out the chorus. Madame Picard took it up on the fiddle.

Ursula's turn. She looked to Jonathan, who nodded. Yes, a simple chord progression, Ursula urged her fingers. She could do this.

She did, and they were off.

The patients clapped. The ward filled with more of the injured, doctors, nurses and volunteers. Ursula stayed inside the music, inside the trio she was making with Rowan's tin whistle and Marie-Madeline's fiddle. They became more daring, changing tempo, challenging her. She adjusted, and even began adding flourishes of her own.

They played another tune, then another. All who were able, danced and the space turned back into a ballroom. Circle dances, line dances. The Canadian musicians knew so many tunes! And Ursula found the chords in all.

Around them, faces were flush with exertion, with happiness. Rowan paused, then began a slower-paced composition. As Ursula played, she realized that this new melody made her want to cry. Stay inside it, she warned her overwhelmed emotions. Give the music your fingers, not your soul.

"Stop." A raspy male voice demanded. "That song is forbidden."

An officer, one of high rank, Ursula could tell by the bars at his shoulders, stood in the doorway.

Rowan cocked his head. "'The Rambling Laborer' is forbidden, sir?" he asked.

"That's not anybody's laborer," a one-legged patient interjected, "it's 'Brighton Camp.'"

"It is neither one of those," the officer insisted. "And, look."

Ursula lifted her head, realizing that her own battle for composure had cut her off from their audience. Most of them were weeping. A one-armed soldier with eyes as grey as his uniform began to sing:

*If ever I travel this road
again
If the Yankees they don't kill
me
I'll go right back to
Tennessee
To the girl I left behind me.*

The officer in the doorway turned his mounting ire on Rowan. "You see? It is that song, the forbidden one. 'The Girl I left Behind Me.' Look around! See what you have done?"

"Done? What have I done?" Rowan echoed.

Captain Cole stepped up to the officer. "Lieutenant Buckley cannot see, Major. This is a ward of the blind and limbless. Do not fear. There will be no desertions because of a song here. These men are going to die or go home."

The major's mouth twitched, before he straightened further. "It can be heard, doctor. Music carries. In the night. On the wind."

With each of his clipped pronouncements he stepped back, as if death or a severed arm or leg was contagious, until he disappeared in the shadows beyond the doorway.

Ursula's fingers ached.

"Thank you, Sister," Rowan said, formally bowing.

She must stop shaking. But the realization was too overwhelming--she would be the one he left behind. Rowan would go home to again be with the women who love him. Not with her, never with her. She must bear up until she could go back, disappear behind the convent walls and her garden.

The song had accomplished what the officer had feared. It had broken her will to fight. It had broken her heart.

* * *

The note on the elegant, embossed card, had come after Sister Philomena had gone to bed in her room at the other end of the long servants' quarters hallway, so Ursula could not consult with her superior. If she'd cared to, and she did not care to. She was a grown woman, not needing a superior's permission to accept an invitation.

As she walked in, Ursula discovered that Madame Picard had made her own tiny quarters a home. All its surfaces and the arms and backs of chairs were covered with intricate lace covers in swirling designs similar to those on her collars and cuffs. On the marble fireplace rested a cobalt blue vase, a chunk of rosin for her bow, and small pictures in silver frames. In Ursula's world, such things were considered vanities, to be purged with all the others when she gave herself to God. The tea had the scent of lemon balm infused within. It calmed her, at least until Madame Picard sat. Her purple gown was so beautifully made. Her hair's silver lights swirled, set off with artful tendrils. Her color was high and vibrant. Ursula felt herself disappearing into her offered chair.

And then the woman's questions began.

"Tell me, Sister. Do you think there is only one path to God?"

"No."

"Eh bien, good. We may talk, then."

Ursula suddenly wanted the safety of her own room. "I am afraid you would not find me a very stimulating conversationalist, Madame."

"And why is that?"

"I have many gaps in my life, in my knowledge of the world. I joined my order many years ago, you see."

"Half your lifetime ago. So your brother has told me."

105

"Has he?" Jonathan. He had not ceased his scheming. "I'm afraid it was an abrupt parting for my brother."

"And not for you?"

"For me too, of course. But Jonathan was only a little boy. He could not understand." Why did her voice waver?

"Do you?"

"Yes. I was guided by a providential hand. I was saved by my choice."

"Choice? Or threat to an obstinate child?"

Ah, Jonathan's idea of what had happened that night. But it sounded different, even wiser, coming from this woman.

"There are seldom only two paths, my dear one," Madame Picard said.

"There were but two for me."

"Perhaps. At the time. Which is not this time. And you are not a girl, dreaming of dances, who did not like the smell of the man her stepfather chose for her."

Ursula placed her teacup down. She stood, noticing the daguerreotype of Madame Picard and two other women, similarly striking, but without their sister's height. "Bourbon. He smelled of bourbon. I do not remember telling Jonathan that."

"Ah, but you did. And he kept everything in his heart. My dear Ursula. You are now a strong, educated woman, thanks to the fallen sister with the angel's name."

"With a debt towards those who made me so."

"A debt? A debt?" Madame took up an image from the fireplace mantle, the framed drawing of the three women at a younger time, with a child among their skirts. "Do you think your order of nuns took you in the way my sisters and I took Rowan? Starved, stricken with his grieving? With only his whistle to help him remember there was still beauty in the world?" The small boy had enormous, haunted eyes. He leaned into the side of a dew-eyed woman.

"Marie Agathe," Madame Picard introduced her. "She loves him with the most ardor, perhaps, but any of us would put our hand in the fire for him, make no mistake.

No, your people were not like us! You were part of a plan, a scheme."

"No."

"Mais oui. To break you toward an early marriage, to have your inheritance enter your stepfather's family. And, at the convent, when you showed devotion to your studies, your plants and remedies, you grew more valuable to the sisters. Why not take a rich yearly fee to keep you caged when, with patience, they will have your lifelong service besides your donated inheritance? If they could succeed in keeping you afraid."

"Afraid?"

"Of this thing that haunts you, makes your eyes so sad, little one. Afraid of your own woman's power."

"Madame Picard. That cannot be."

"Think on it. With that mind they themselves helped you to develop. They desire you for their own. Your brother has grown wise, my dear. He wishes to give you another choice. Are you brave enough for that?"

A choice? What would she do with such a choice? She could only see Rowan, and behind him, her stepfather ready to cut him down, the way he cut down Sling. No. Another image, quickly, she begged her mind's eye. One came, of her garden, full of angelica, lemon balm, as it was before the fire. Then she could breathe again. And speak.

"I promised myself to God, Madame."

"Yes. You ran away. As Rowan did, from the Great Hunger. But he ran toward, as well."

"Toward you and your sisters."

"Yes. But we did not turn him into one of us when we taught him our language, our ways. We did not change his name, or try to make him forget who he was. This the sisters would do with you, I think. They will tell themselves it is for the glory of God. Some, like Sister Philomena, have even come to believe it, I think. They are the most dangerous, the believers, who hear the call of heaven in their scheming."

"I cannot leave them."

Madame Picard rose, borrowed light from the fire with a paper spill and lit a candle at the small desk, then on the table. Even her shadow was beautiful as she refilled their cups with her tea.

"Think. Is not free will one of God's blessings, my dear? Our Rowan, when he grew into his manhood, he ran to yet another country, your country, in the time of its greatest danger. Joined an army because of what he cherishes. All from that sacred part of him, his free will. This broke our hearts, this will of his--do not mistake. We, my sisters and I, we know what war is, what it is doing to him. But we bid him adieu, with sorrow but not anger, because that is what deep love allows."

"And in repayment, my country left him for dead." Ursula reached across the table, squeezed Madame Picard's hands between hers. "You must take him home, Madame Picard. He is too good for us," she whispered, before she rose to go.

* * *

Later that night, when Ursula had undressed down to her shift, she heard a tapping at her room's door. It must be the white cat who had attached herself to their ward, scratching for one more scrap. Well, the creature was a good mouser. Ursula didn't even bother wrapping herself in her shawl before opening the door.

To another stray, Rowan Buckley.

Standing there, filling her doorway, without even the elegant walking stick Jonathan had bought for him.

"Rowan," she pronounced, feeling the breeze of the hallway on her shoulders. Cold. Too cold for him. "Who is with you?"

"No one."

"Then how did you—?"

"Ursula. Let me in. Please."

Did Jonathan lead him here? Or did Rowan have the third floor's servant rooms and hallways memorized? No matter. Suffering. There was such suffering in his face. And something else, a bristling anger. It did not frighten her, the way her stepfather's anger frightened her.

She took his hand. "Come," she whispered as calmly as she could, given the current she felt ignite upon contact.

He needed her, for something. Perhaps even to give him permission to hate her. She forced herself to breathe as she led him toward her lone chair. When she touched his shoulder to signal its presence behind him, he took up that hand and held it against the curve of his face, the undamaged side, so handsome in the lamplight.

She felt a fullness swell her being. She need never fear this man, it told her. And what else? That she loved him. That she would always love him. That she wanted, even now, to guide those sensitive musician's fingers of his along her neck, her bare arms, so he might know how little clothing was between them. Siren. She heard her stepfather's voice.

No, there was no danger of seduction. For Rowan Buckley knew her now. Knew her to be a liar.

As if sensing her thoughts, Rowan released her hand abruptly, and sat.

She knelt before him, needing his heat more than her shawl or her fire, even here in November. Rowan stared straight ahead, as if he had not heard her movement, did not know where she was, or did not want to know.

"Ursula," he breathed out her given name again. He was trying to be stern, she realized, and failing. The suffering crept into his voice. "Why did you not tell me?"

His question demanded the truth.

"Because I did not want to disappear," she admitted to him, and to herself.

"Disappear?" His head came down at last toward her voice.

"Rowan. After the battle. You were the only one who knew when it was I who tended you. I, and not one of the other sisters. Imagine that? Only you, who cannot see. And you had such a clear sense of me, that…"

"That what?" he demanded.

"Do not make me say it, I am so ashamed! It is my great failing, and a sin of pride. And it has led to this. I am not supposed to mind."

He leaned over until their noses were almost touching. "Mind what? Being invisible?"

"Yes."

He ran his fingers over hers, tracing her palms, her knuckles, her joints. Her already heightened senses thrummed.

Did he not despise her, then?

His hands found her face and held it before him.

"Listen to me, Ursula. I have seen terrible things, in my homeland, on Grosse Isle, in this war. Things no one should see. But you? Invisible? You are a beauty of God's creation, my protector bear. Making you invisible is among the blackest of sins, surely."

Slowly, his fingers traced the bones of her face. Her breath caught. She closed her eyes, but that could not hold back the tears. How was it the more she tried to drive him away with confessions of her grievous faults, the closer he came, the sweeter things he said?

Now he was making soft, clicking sounds of comfort. This exquisite tenderness was not what she deserved. She lifted her head, to get more air. Not to feel his breath, flavored with mint.

He closed his lid over his eye. "I see you," he said. "I always will, no matter our circumstances. Whisper my name, and I will find you, though you stand among millions."

His eye appeared again, met hers, locked there, steady, focused. A trick of the imperfect light, of course. She felt suspended there, in that light.

"I miss you."

Which of them said that? She'd better say it too, in case it had been he.

When she did, he smiled.

And then it was the same, between them, the same intense longing.

He rose to his feet, brought her with him. He pressed her up against the warm bricks of the hearth, as if this was the last night of time itself and they were at the end of the universe.

He kissed her hard and long and deep. He lifted her to her high medicine table and sat her there without disturbing a bottle, a jar. She kicked her legs, like a child. He laughed against her neck and she felt the tuft of beard that had returned beneath his bottom lip. That beard made her long to do what she did now, flick her tongue out to lick it like a mother cat.

"Never invisible, Ursa," he whispered.

"Rowan," she breathed at his ear, "forgive me for desiring this."

He kissed her cheek, then her jaw, then her mouth. Did sighted men kiss so tenderly?

"There is no fault here, in this, love."

Rowan's hands massaged that place behind her ears, the place which always felt strained after hours of bending over patients.

And then, another sweet whisper, there, against her ear. "Let us always keep forgiveness between us. It may someday be all we have."

"Yes, good," she breathed, not understanding what she was agreeing to, only wanting so much, each of these things he did, and then what she did, to cause those fine gasps of pleasure out of his mouth, against her skin.

Her shift pooled at her hips when he entered her, more sounds bursting at her ear. It was not his nasal, expert French, the same way Madame Picard spoke it. This must be his other language, the Irish one, its phrasing hushed, full of wonder, like prayer. And it must be blasphemy even thinking such things about a pagan tongue, as they did these pagan things that gave such wanton pleasure. The fleeting thought was the last remnant of her shame as he moved in, out, and she was then beyond thinking at all.

Her senses came together, compressed, flew. Where? To the bed, that's where they were now, but she did not know how they had arrived. She knew nothing beyond the feel of him: slick, gliding. Hard and tender, all at once. She became the peaking sensation just before she collapsed, gasping against the planes of his chest.

When she opened her eyes again they were snug in her narrow bed, his heartbeat almost normal at her ear. He murmured, covering them both with the soft beautifully worked quilt that the last tenant of the room, the grievously ill spinster nurse from Massachusetts, had left to her.

They said she was dying, but Ursula did not think so. The nurse had pressed her foxglove salve into Ursula's hands at the train station, along with the quilt, before her family took her home. But she still had such fire in her suffering eyes. Now, Ursula thought, if she and Rowan had to stay here under Miss Alcott's quilt forever, she would not mind. She could live within the heartbeat of this man who had replaced so many years of loneliness with joy.

But when Ursula opened her eyes again, Rowan was gone, with only one tipped-over bottle of licorice-flavored tonic on her medicine table the evidence of his visit.

Chapter 21

"Nice collection of baubles," Fish remarked.

"Keep away from those eyes!" Captain Cole warned him.

"Need not be testy, doctor!" Lake defended his compatriot. "Thad's only curious."

"And ham-hocked." Captain Cole kept his gaze guarding the compartmentalized box. Inside were finely-crafted artifacts that shone with a clarity that rivaled the brilliance of their human counterparts.

Captain Cole seemed as uncomfortable as Rowan was with this spying business. Spies were liars, and liars had to keep darting around, to keep their victims off balance, distracted, so they did not notice the deceptions. Or maybe Fisher, Lake and their leader Goss were bad spies, and nervous. Pain started back behind Rowan's patched eye socket, from trying to keep the three constantly moving men in his limited sight lines.

Dr. Cole stopped the agent Fisher's second grab for one of the glass eyes his mother had sent from the German ocularist in New York. "Out!" he shouted. "To the balcony, the pack of you until my session with Lieutenant Buckley has concluded!"

The three men stared at Captain Cole, a formidable pronged instrument poised in his grip, before retreating without protest.

Once the doors were closed, the doctor's sternness evaporated.

"What they think I am about to do to you with these rib shears, I'll never know," he admitted, "But I am glad they have served the purpose of ridding us of that crew. Now, before they freeze out there, let us finish." He placed the instrument back in his velvet lined case.

It was a vanity, being fitted for a glass eye, Rowan thought. He would just as soon keep wearing the patch. Ursula loved him as he was.

Ursula loved him. The miracle of it made all things possible. And the possibilities were now occupying many of his waking moments. Once he managed to free her of his army's suspicion, he'd convince her to marry him and send her home with Marie Madeline. Then he'd leave off this spying business and find Captain Merritt and what was left of his company, and try to keep his men and himself alive until this blasted country hauled itself together again.

He had plans. A dangerous thing for a soldier at war, he knew. But he loved the mere thought of a future with his great protector bear, his deeply loved Callisto.

"Look into the light if you would, Lieutenant," Captain Cole directed.

"You have patients in more dire need, sir, if you don't mind me saying so."

"I like to finish projects. Few turn out so well. Now to the left, please. Yes," he said, holding the eye to the hard winter light from the window, "I believe this is the closest we can get, given that propensity of your eye's color to shift with your surroundings. I'd advise a wardrobe where blue continues to predominate. And a climate of cloudless skies."

Rowan laughed. "My home will provide, sir."

Ursula would love the farm at Lacolle. So would their children. Healthy, strong, never-hungry children.

He was way ahead of himself again.

Last night, he had only meant to ask her the question that bothered him so. Why had she not told him she was married to God, and unattainable? That question answered only, to keep the wound between them from festering.

He did not expect Ursula to look so beautiful, dressed in one layer only, and still innocent of her effect on him, because of the damnable lie about his returned sight.

And then, her answer. How could that not melt the hardest heart?

She did not want to disappear? Rowan had not thought a woman could fear such a thing. They were all so beautiful. How had Ursula not laughed at him, a one-eyed soldier, saying such things as being able to find her among millions?

But she had not laughed. She had glowed in her wonder. And when he kissed her, she had returned his passion. Then they were undone, again, there in the shadows of the small room scented with the richness of her, and the lavender scent of the well-made quit on her bed.

Was not this enjoyment God's gift? And now she was his, surely? For their time was no mistake born of a misty night and the drink.

Yes. She was his.

"Almost complete, Lieutenant. Are you well?" Captain Cole called him from his thoughts.

"Very well, sir, thank you."

Would they understand— Marie Madeline, Jonathan and Ursula? About the spying? About why he had lied to them, so that he could free her from their notions of treason? Could he use his storytelling gift to get them to laugh about the humorless Major Goss, about the hapless spies Fisher and Lake and their scheme? These people he loved, they would forgive him, and years from now they would have a good war story, an antidote for all the sorrowful ones.

"There. I hope it meets with your approval."

The looking glass Dr. Cole put before him reflected a face that the blue glass eye somehow balanced again. He recognized the reflection as his own.

The sight of him was not as it had been, of course. It was now scarred and rough and bruised about his healing nose, but it might not frighten children. Good.

Rowan's pleasure must have shown, because the doctor was beaming.

"I believe my assistant would call you a good healer, Lieutenant," he said, "to have come back to us from such a devastating injury."

Rowan looked past the doctor. His functioning eye slowly focused beyond the glass doors, where Fisher and Lake were taking the air with their superior Major Goss on one of the grand house's many balconies. He returned his gaze as the patiently waiting Captain Cole came into sharp focus.

Rowan had never before thought about what a miracle sight is. He hoped he would never forget. There, alone with the kind-hearted physician, he allowed unbidden words to fly through his mouth.

"I love Sister Ursula, sir."

"Yes, Lieutenant, I know."

"Do you think looking like this is enough? Do you think she will have me?"

Captain Cole smiled. "As a Congregationalist, I am not familiar with the tenants of your faith, and the difficulties her veil presents to your marriage. But I think you should not wait too long to ask." He nodded toward the balcony doors. "Now, I fear we must return Sword, Famine, and Plague to our presence before I will have to treat their frostbite. I'll leave you to them and their latest scheme. And have Tom get your bed ready. You'll need some rest after your session with them."

* * *

Major Goss came through the balcony doors in time to watch Doctor Cole's disappearing form. "Now where is he going? That man is a disgrace to his uniform!"

"It is fortunate for his patients that his superiors do not share your opinion," sir," Rowan said quietly.

"You are hardly better, nursed by both Canadians that have not been properly interviewed regarding their stance on the war, and suspect Marylanders besides!"

Lake and Fisher nodded their fellow disapproval together.

"Major Goss," Rowan tried in his most patient voice, "surely it is time for you to move on. You have seen how your suspects treat patients of both North and South with respect and dignity no matter which side caused their wounds."

"Move on? Who are you to question our actions? My associates and I are not green recruits that you must turn into fighting men, sir! Kindly report on your observations of the last three days."

Rowan straightened himself in the intricately carved ladder back chair. "Wednesday, despite dutifully producing his laudable pus, Major Hawley passed from this life just before dawn. Colonel Blanchard from Carolina continues to improve at both his hand wound and card game winnings with officers of both sides. On Thursday—"

"Which Carolina?"

"Sir?

"From which Carolina, North or South, is Colonel Blanchard?"

"I don't know."

"Do you hear that? He does not know!" Goss proclaimed in disgust to his jackals, before dead-eying Rowan. "Our chief suspect is no longer in your thrall, sir. Have you not seen it with your imperfect vision? Surely you have noticed the attention Colonel Blanchard has exhibited for our younger sister of mercy from Maryland?"

"I have noticed," Rowan said evenly. The officer was handsome and charming and displayed the attitude of a rich man used to having his way with women. He had even gotten Sister Philomena smiling as she came up from the kitchen, putting jars of preserves and writing papers into his hands. It mattered not a whit, the colonel's way with women. Ursula and he belonged to each other.

"You will learn all you can about Colonel Blanchard, Lieutenant, and you will listen well to the conversations he has with Sister Ursula Kingsley. For they share a past at critical crossroads of this investigation."

"What are you saying?"

"Troop location information about the Army of the Potomac. Delivered to the other side. This information came out of the last place Sister Ursula attended Colonel Blanchard— the Mother House. And our planted information continues slipping out, from here. Have I made myself quite clear?"

Of course. At the convent, Ursula was always being called upstairs to work with those who were not dying. Blanchard and his cold eyes was one of them. Time to banish future thoughts out of his love-sick mind and get to work. Because the charming Colonel Blanchard talked with everyone. Learn his card games. Watch him. "Yes, sir," he told his commanding officer.

* * *

Once Rowan was back on the ward and under the covers of his corner-set bed, his doctor leaned over him. "Now that the socket is getting used to its new inhabitant, we will keep watch to make sure an infection does not develop. And then— "

"My petit frere will be discharged so I might bring him home, no?" Marie Madeleine finished Captain Cole's sentence as she stared down the three government men.

Rowan turned. She looked so pleased with the prospect of his release from the army. He was heartily sick of playing blind.

"Well, Madame," Captain Cole hedged, "I fear our army moves more slowly than you would prefer in dismissing good soldiers."

Marie Madeline fisted her hands at her long waist. Rowan wished again that the lot had fallen to the more diplomatic Marie Catherine as the eldest of the three Belanger sisters began her tirade. She set her sights on Major Goss first.

"And how can a sightless man be a soldier, sir? Has my brother not given enough to your warring country? Surely we will have permission to take our leave?"

118

"It is not for me to say. This man is in Captain Cole's care."

Ursula entered the ward, a basin in her hand. Would she renounce her vows and take new ones, binding her to him? Rowan would know her answer soon. He hoped he had the courage to accept it.

The colonel from one of the Carolinas called her to his bedside before she reached the escalating argument being waged around Rowan. Quebecois words began popping out of Marie-Madeline like birdshot, aimed at Dr. Cole. Rowan took her hand, held it against his heart. He wanted to tell her that arguments were useless, because he was not blind, and would not be going home.

The gesture only agitated Marie Madeline further. Dr. Cole begged her to speak more slowly, as his French was not as good as hers. Rowan sighed hard and turned his attention back to Ursula and the Colonel. Blanchfield? Blanchard, Colonel Blanchard from the Carolina he was supposed to ferret out, though he'd yet to exchange more than a few pleasantries with the man.

The patient had Ursula pulled low, her ear to his mouth. She shook her head, spoke a few words. What was she saying? Marie Madeline's heated argument would not allow Rowan to hear.

Blanchard laughed. Ursula's shoulders relaxed. She nodded, smiling. Rowan felt a stab of jealousy as she stayed close to the officer, as she drew the scissors from her pocket. Was that their discussion? Damn the man. Did he ask her to trim his flaxen locks?

The glint of the blades flashed.

Blanchard suddenly snatched them into his bandaged hand, forced Ursula to her knees, and held them opened at her throat. She gasped. He pressed.

Rowan reached into the Zouave jacket hanging from his bedpost, retrieved the pistol, cocked its hammer.

A taunting voice inside invited him to watch his dreams die, again.

The Southern officer swung back the blades. Rowan knew the gesture, point angled towards the center back of the neck. He'd trained his own troops in it: cutting through veins, arteries, giving a swift death to the enemy. Rowan aimed, fired.

The eyes below the small, newly-made red hole lost focus. The grip at Ursula's throat lost its power. The scissors clattered to the floorboards. The southern colonel fell back on the blue striped coverlet.

Silence, at last. Ringing, echoing, silence. Rowan watched blood trickle down Ursula's starched white collar. Watched her horrified eyes glaze over.

Then time resumed in all its fury, so fast Rowan struggled to keep track of what was happening: Ursula surrounded by Lake, Fisher and Major Goss. Goss peppering her with questions as she covered her ears. Her superior, Sister Philomena, framed in hall doorway, then standing before Rowan, hauling back and slapping his face as she screamed, "Murderer!"

Enough. He cleared her from his sightline, then fought his way to Ursula, lifted her off her feet. She reached for his burning cheek. Cold. Her touch was too cold.

"Rowan. You can see," she said.

"Yes."

He had to make her warmer. Where was Dr. Cole? He would know what to do. But before he could find him, the voice of Major Goss rang out. "Lieutenant Buckley. You will halt where your stand, sir! That woman is under arrest."

Chapter 22

Georgetown, The Custis Mansion

Like the hospital, the prison had once been a fine home. It was still formally appointed, although the small office room was bare of all but necessary furniture: a bookcase, three chairs, a substantial carved desk. Rowan sat behind the desk, across from his own beloved Marie-Madeline, the first of three appointed conversations his superiors had placed on his "schedule." How he hated his life as an officer thus far.

"I am thankful to Our Lord and his dear Mother for your returned sight," she began, as if he was a stranger.

"Marie Madeline, I am a soldier. Under orders."

"To deceive your own family?"

"Yes."

"These are unholy orders."

"Maybe."

"There is no may be! I am treated like...like le malfaiteur, oh, what is the English?

"A criminal."

"Just so! And your woman, your sweet and loving woman, is now here in this place, under guard! What have we accomplished, she and I, except to serve you foolish men at war?"

"None of this is my doing."

Her sharp eyes took in the room. "And yet you have a place here. And power." She rose to her full height, rounded the desk and approached his chair. She grabbed his jaw suddenly, holding him in that hand. "Power you must use, my darling boy," she whispered. "Rowan, it was most difficult, I know, taking a life. But it preserved that of your woman. And I am so happy that you are able to see again. Vraiment. Look past this foolish thing, my anger. You will even be your handsome self again, I think. But here, now, you must find the wit to set your woman free. This war, this city of deceptions will eat her whole. Get her to the farm, to us. We will care for her, I promise. We will love her. We will keep her well."

She released him at last.

"Another orphan?" he whispered.

She smiled at last. "Or two, or three, if your harvest is good, eh? There is life in us yet for this, my sisters and me, for this. Send her north."

"I do not know how."

"Not yet. But you have an ally in her brother. If you can get back in his graces. He has just now arrived to be granted the next audience with you. I leave you to him, petit frère"

Rowan steeled himself, the way he did in battle waiting for the sound of that blood-chilling rebel yell. Still, he felt his stomach clench as Jonathan Kingsley stomped into the room, smelling of horse, leather, and whiskey.

Ursula's brother paced around the table, a blur of sharp turns, until Rowan preferred hearing that rebel yell.

What he got, finally, was a soft, drawling rage. "I ought to call you out."

"Marie Madeline has already done that. And I suspect she's a better shot."

"Those idiots out there, they threaten to haul that formidable woman back to Canada!"

"I know," Rowan admitted softly.

"You must not allow this! We need her, although I would be happy to take her place behind dueling pistols and kill you!"

"And what good would that do?"

"If I am lucky, relieve this miserable city of one more scoundrel. Lieutenant." Rowan's new rank was now on public display thanks to having a private seamstress in Marie-Madeline at his uniform. Jonathan stopped his pacing only long enough to sneer. "Look at you now. No longer our humble Sergeant. A Yankee officer. Feigning blindness and seducing my sister."

"You know better."

"Do I? You work for those who imprison her now, do you not? Have we earned you your new commission? Ferreting out the Maryland spies? And why I am not in irons as well?"

"Ursula is not in irons, Jonathan."

"And for that I am in your debt?"

The younger man bowed his head, leaned on the table between them, then ran his hand through his golden curls. "My God, Rowan. I am cast adrift without a rudder. What in hell is going on?"

His given name. At last. Testifying that their frayed friendship was somehow holding. "That's a question we both desire answered." Rowan gestured toward the chair. "You are making me dizzy. Will you sit?"

Jonathan threw his hat down and slumped his itching petulance into the shield back chair.

Rowan moved his matching chair across from Ursula's brother and sat. "What have they told you?"

"That my sister is suspected of spying for the Confederacy. You allowed it, Rowan. You allowed them take her here."

"I had no power to prevent it."

"My sister lived inside a convent's walls until, by an accident of geography, she was drawn into nursing the likes of you. Your superiors can neither lead men nor recognize spies!" Rowan's pained expression earned him a louder outburst. "There, now! Does that statement make me disloyal to the precious Union? The Union that is tearing my country to bloody shreds?"

"Jonathan, stop." Rowan summoned him silent with his sergeant voice.

He kept his tired eye focused on his friend's face. Jonathan Kingsley was so young, like the new recruits sent to him for training before battle seared and seasoned them. Bright-minded, like most of them.

Was Jonathan unnerved by his returned sight? Use it. Stare hard. Pound some sense into him before the men listening to their conversation judged him sufficiently treasonous to lock him away too.

"These outbursts will not help her."

"Now you sound like my father."

"Father?"

"Yes. He's traveled directly behind me on the road here."

"Why?"

"Surely to make things worse." He looked down at his hands. "Rowan, what will help my sister?" he asked.

Yes, very young. And why Rowan himself must stay calm, put aside his questions about this complication, this father. Because here, now, his superiors might misinterpret Jonathan's desperation. They might not recognize the goodness that was at its heart.

Rowan took a breath. "They have not given us much time, so I need for you to listen well. I was ordered to keep my returned sight from all but the government men and Doctor Cole and his assistant. Because, yes, I am assigned to discover how troop location information is being passed behind enemy lines. They think the source was a patient who I killed yesterday."

Jonathan raised his head. "You killed a patient?"

"He threatened your sister's life. I was not waiting for the blade to cut further."

"Rowan—"

"Listen. Please. They are now holding Ursula because they found a ciphered message in her quarters. And because your sister and this officer were talking before he held the scissors to her throat."

"Scissors? Throat? Is she hurt?"

"A small wound." Admitting his failure to her brother pained him. Do not show it. Keep talking. "Dr. Cole said it should not be causing—"

"Causing what? What does Ursula say about all this?"

"That is what I am trying to tell you. Ursula has not spoken."

"She will not speak in her own defense?"

"No. Dr. Cole believes she cannot, though not from the injury done her. The shock of what happened he says may be the cause. Jonathan, do you remember any other time when she could not speak?"

"Yes. Let me see her. I need to see her."

"I think they will allow it. If I am with you." Rowan moved closer and whispered against his shoulder. "They will be watching, and listening."

"As they are now?"

"Yes. They will show you to her quarters," Rowan directed, louder. "Wait there for me."

Jonathan rubbed a smudge of dirt off his chin with the back of his hand. "All right." He took a step for the door, then turned. "On the battlefield, and at the convent. Were you a spy then?"

"No."

Jonathan looked more deeply into Rowan's face, assessing both eyes, the sighted and the glass one. "Dr. Cole. He does good work."

"Yes."

Slowly, Ursula's brother offered Rowan his hand.

"Thank you. For what you did for my sister."

"I love her, Jonathan. That will not change."

It would not, were she to betray him every day of his life, Rowan realized. It was a powerful bond. And it could be the ruin of both their families.

Chapter 23

As two guards led Jonathan up the winding stairs to wait to see his sister, two others walked Rowan back to his office. The elder Kingsley and Sister Philomena were brought into the room. The scent of horses ridden too fast and too hard came with them. The man's hooded eyes took a lengthy assessment of Rowan. As he returned the gaze, Rowan saw little resemblance, father to son. This man was barrel-chested, with a heavily muscled frame. He had none of Jonathan's careless, easy grace. Everything about him was practiced, precise, heavy. Is that what drew Ursula's mother, a grieving widow to this man— how substantial and grounded he was? Sister Philomena stared at the ribbon patterned in the carpeting. Both ignored the waiting chairs, but at least Kingsley looked at him.

"Lieutenant Buckley, my son fancies himself your great friend." The Maryland planter said Rowan's officer's rank with a disapproving edge. Or did he imagine it? "I hope you will also allow his father some of your good counsel."

Good counsel? Not what Rowan expected, or the rich warmth that entered the man's tone. Magnus Kingsley walked out of Rowan's limited line of sight, making him turn his head. Watch. Listen. He knew how to do both, instincts were bred in the bones of the Irish poor.

"Her mother and I thought she would be safe, away from the world, doing good, simple work among the sisters." He nodded to his silent companion, Sister Philomena. "Then the horrors of this war invaded her peace, her sanctuary," he continued. "Is that not correct, Sister?"

Sister Philomena raised her head, but her cold stare only reached Rowan's shoulder. She held her red and raw hands before her waist, clenching, then unclenching her fingers. Rowan had the feeling that she'd like that energy pressed around his throat.

"We believe her mind is ravaged again," she said in a hoarse whisper.

"Again?" Rowan demanded.

Magnus Kingsley stepped forward. "Did my son not tell you? Of course he would not. He sees his sister through a child's eyes, before her change. The plain truth is that Ursula has been prone to a...delicate state of mind," his father said. "The sisters understand, and have been so kind. There is a family history of derangement on her father's side. It is even said that his own demise was...well, no use speculating over the long departed, whatever the circumstances."

What was going on here? Rowan wished Jonathan was beside him.

"Have you not observed the fragile nature of her sensibilities yourself, Lieutenant Buckley?"

"I have not, sir." Stop. Give nothing away, even to defend her.

Magnus Kingsley smiled without humor.

"But of course, you were severely injured, and before that used to a more simple way of life. Well. I admire your devotion, sir. And your loyalty in the face of these charges of conspiring with the enemy. Our dear Ursula has three champions now. We must keep her safe, do you not agree?"

"Yes. On that we agree."

"Prison is not the place for her, is it? Perhaps someone took advantage of her innocent, ignorant nature to draw her into a disloyal scheme. But if we all testified before Major Goss and his superiors together, as to the unsound nature of her mind, perhaps then they will agree to have us quietly take her away. Not back to the convent, of course. My daughter has brought suspicion and disgrace down upon the motherhouse, I fear."

He nodded and Sister Philomena spoke again. "I spoke with the bishop himself about her return," she said, "but to no good purpose, not at his time."

"And we appreciate your efforts, Sister, do we not, Lieutenant?" Kingsley said. "Well, it matters not. Released from here, I will make sure she is comfortably ensconced."

"Ensconced?" Rowan meant to sound curious only, but felt his jaw tightening with effort.

"Enrolled, if you will. In a quiet place, with good, compassionate care and treatments."

Rowan kept his voice mild. "Would this course of action also have your son's support, Mr. Kingsley?"

A bead of sweat lined one of the creases in his high forehead. There, a resemblance with Jonathan, the high forehead. "My misguided son will always see his sister, teacher and playmate snatched away from him. Do not concern yourself. He will come around to our way of thinking of her in good time, Lieutenant."

"But the case would be stronger," Rowan leaned harder on his Canadian backwoods cadence, "if there was full family agreement, eh?"

"I hardly think that likely."

"You never know. I'd best talk with him on this matter."

Magnus Kingsley's sweat glistened now. "I doubt you could change his mind."

Silence, charged between them.

This man, a slaveholder from a border state, and an abductor of freemen according to Jonathan, had no power here, not even over his recently come-of-age son. Did he know it? Yes. Finally, the elder Kingsley made a deep bow from his waist. "But, of course I have no objection, if you think it is a prudent course of action."

"I do, sir."

"You cannot allow it. You must not. She will be dead within a year in a place like that. If she does not take refuge in the madness around her."

Rowan steadied his hand at Jonathan's shoulder. It finally stopped his movement, there in the antechamber leading to Ursula's guarded quarters. "I know, I know. Hush now."

His own mind was racing. He had to work at slowing his own breathing. He wanted to break her out, even if it would mean a renegade lifetime for them both. More likely he'd be shot for a traitor and she'd wind up in the asylum anyway. Think. Think more clearly. But nothing was coming to him.

"I don't know what to do," he voiced his terror aloud.

To his astonishment, Jonathan Kingsley smiled. "Maybe you have already done it."

"What have I done?"

"Gotten us down to our ace."

"Ace?"

"I am keeping it ensconced, of course, as you are so damned honorable."

Jonathan took the folded paper from a pocket inside his high, scuffed brown boot. He grinned, looking about the age of twelve. "That man downstairs, he is not her father. He has no legal hold on her. But you do. You have married her."

Chapter 24

"That is ridiculous."

"Signed and registered. Not a church wedding of course. But we have to make do in wartime," Jonathan said as he opened the document.

Rowan noticed the date and recognized his own scrawl next to Ursula's elegant signature. "What in hell is this?"

"Well, now. You did not ask such belligerent questions at the time. I told you we needed this favor and you happily obliged."

"When?"

"The night they took you away from us, brought you to Washington. You know, I might have liked you better then, tattered, bandaged up and blind. Did they make you a lieutenant because you spied on us?"

Rowan took the document from Jonathan Kingsley's hand. Yes. He had been addled by morphine, but he remembered scraping the pen across thick vellum surface. Something official and important, he'd thought.

He lifted his head. "Will this stand?"

Jonathan sneered. "This is Washington city, country boy. Everything has a price here. It had better stand." He sniffed. "The bribes cost me my best racing horse."

The black ink stared at Rowan, daring him to protest further. His families, both the Irish one and the Maries, did not raise a foolish man. One who knew a gift when he saw one. He remembered the night of the peach scented brandy, and the feel of her skin in the moonlight.

"Do not look so all-fired pleased with yourself," Jonathan Kingsley warned. "Remember, this was my doing. Ursula has not married you back yet."

"But, right here. She has signed it."

"Not…strictly speaking."

"Jonathan—"

"She taught me to write. So I have known her signature as well as my own since I was five. Yes, I forged it."

Rowan's breath caught.

"Now, do not get all honorable! Admit that my ability to impersonate her Spencerian script came in damned handy now that even you are out of ideas! Buck up, kinsman! Time to get back down there with your superiors. Assert your rights as a husband and do some dealing with that glib tongue of yours. Let's get her out of here."

* * *

It was like the parlor of the Marie's, where the best furniture was, where tea and hard bargaining awaited all tradesmen. As he stood beside her brother, Rowan looked across the room, recognizing the weave of the plain black dress and its simple white collar as one of Marie Madeline's, carefully refitted to Ursula's smaller proportions. There was something else, more structured about the way she appeared now, too, at her middle. A corset. The thin bandage around Ursula's neck almost looked like an ornament. Her head was covered by a simple lace cap. In another time and place, he would have rejoiced, seeing her dressed like this, like a woman and not a nun.

Ursula's attention was still on the opened book.

Beside him, Jonathan twitched, drew in a breath. Rowan touched his arm. "Softly," he breathed out to her brother.

"Ursula," Jonathan called.

She turned. The suffering in her eyes eased until she shifted her attention to Rowan. Then it returned, intensified. Her hand reached to her throat.

Tainted. He was tainted now, Rowan thought, with both death and deception. So he stood by the door, intentionally blocking the small opening the government men had bored into its paneled chestnut to spy on her. It was a clumsy effort that had now marred the elegant sitting

131

room forever. But he could place himself before it and provide some privacy, at least.

Jonathan approached, knelt beside Ursula. "It was not your fault," he said in a soft voice that Rowan didn't think his fiery temperament could maintain. "You are the sinned against, not the sinning."

She shook her head, looked down at their clasped hands, and wept.

"Yes, yes," he argued with her unspoken protests, "It was ever so, my darling."

Her hand went into his hair, fingers threading through the strands. A comforting gesture, as if Jonathan were a child. What had happened before that other time she had refused to speak? What was the burden of grief Rowan had always sensed from her?

Jonathan exhaled a short laugh. "He is in misery over there, our great blockhead of a patient. Confused. His usual state, perhaps. He needs us, Ursula. Now he thinks we do not care for him anymore, because of his deception to us about his sight, and that you were hurt, and because he could not keep his superiors from arresting you. Of course, if that's the way of it, if you no longer care for him, I certainly will not bother—"

There was a quick movement, like the pounce of a hawk. Jonathan twisted out of her tightening grasp of his hair. "Hey, visit your wrath on him for a change, will you? I shall stand guard."

He rose and kissed her temple before strolling back to Rowan's post. "I shall man the peephole, kin," he offered. "Have a go."

Over the long walk to her side, Rowan noticed that the book on the table was a well-worn bible, open, its bookmark lodged in the Psalms. Her scent, healing lemon balm, finally helped him take in longer, deeper breaths, though he still felt like what he was: confused, awkward, knock-kneed, and, what had Jonathan called him? Block-headed.

Finally he looked into her eyes. Their seas of sorrow engulfed him.

Following her brother's example, he waited until she touched his hand before he knelt before her.

He should speak. But he did not know what to say in the face of such suffering.

She looked over his head, to her brother. Then her free hand took an exquisite, gentle hold of the damaged side of his face before she leaned over and kissed him.

His mouth fell open in shock and the kiss deepened, intensified, burning off whatever fear, animosity, suspicion there was between them. She spoke to him, inside that kiss, banishing his doubts, letting him feel the purity of her love, her gratitude, her forgiveness of his deception. He even felt her rejoicing at his returned sight. Rowan wanted to live there, inside that kiss.

But they ended it together, before he rested his forehead in their clasped hands.

Finally, he found some words. "They will not take you back. At the convent. But you will be free of here soon. I promised to send you north, with Marie Madeline, to the farm of the Maries. To my home, in Canada.

Her fine brow raised.

"I'd best start at the beginning, shall I, then? Ursula, Jonathan and Marie Madeline and I, we agreed, that we have to get you away. We…Jonathan and I, we told them that I married you. And that I would take responsibility for you. So you would be on parole. If you both sign a loyalty oath, and you and Jonathan lease over your home on the Maryland shore for the use of the army and the Union cause. They say if I then send you to Canada for the duration of the war, well, nothing worse than that exile would happen. Those are the conditions we worked out with them. Jonathan and Marie Madeline and I. Do you think you could do that, Ursa Major? Sign the loyalty paper for the federal men and—"

Her nails dug into his palms, her breaths came in short bursts.

She did not speak, but he answered anyway.

"Do not concern yourself with me. I do not care what any of them think of me. I did not seek their damned commission to officer. They can take it away and put me back in sergeant stripes, or as I enlisted, a private. Marie Madeline will help you get settled. And you will like the other Maries, they are not so loud and full of opinions and pronouncements as Marie Madeline is. And you like her anyway, do you not, love? I have a little money, and I will send you more, once I am back at the fighting."

Her eyes widened, her hand flew up to his face, cleared the hair that had fallen over his forehead.

"Oh, now. There are plenty of one-eyed men still in the army. This spying business does not suit me at all. I am better at turning raw recruits into soldiers."

She made a strange sound, like a rusty gate swinging closed as she shook her head. The words came out of her slowly, like birds hatching.

"You take care of them."

"My men? Yes, well, that too, as best I can," he rattled on, when he only wanted to hear her say something else, anything else. "Ursula. You must start over, in my country. Everything will be new. Do you think you could do that?"

"Yes."

There, good. Another word. And she was agreeing with him.

"About the being married. It need not be, that is to say, you can decide about that, after the war is done, and you are safe."

"We," she breathed.

"Yes, well, of course. We will decide."

Her lips touched his knuckles, pressed.

"Now, now," he whispered gruffly, trusting nothing else that might come out of his mouth.

But the harsh voices, then the angry pounding at the door, prevented it. By the time the door gave way, knocking Jonathan to the ground, Rowan was on his feet, guarding her.

Chapter 25

Magnus Kingsley's form filled the door's frame.

Rowan felt Ursula's strong nurse's fingers take hold of his wrist, squeeze. When he looked down on her, the grip left abruptly. Her face lost all its life, and became an empty mask.

"Seducer! Not content to bury yourself alive? Still disgracing your family? What do you think you are doing now?" her stepfather demanded.

Rowan stopped the man's advance. "You will not address my wife in that fashion, sir."

"Wife? It is not possible!"

"It is both possible and done," Jonathan said quietly.

"You. I regret the day the seed left my body and caused you."

"So do I."

Two soldiers appeared and on Rowan's signal, flanked Ursula's stepfather. One offered him his hat and gloves. The elder Kingsley ignored them.

"You are more clever than you look, Irishman," he said. "You and my son have schemed together to separate this strumpet from both family and church, have you? But you do not fully consider the bonds and power of both. This will not stand. A hundred times over you will regret your interference." He took a step into Ursula's line of sight. "As for you, my girl—"

Jonathan sprang. Rowan was quicker and held the younger man back before the soldiers escorted the elder Kingsley from the room.

Rowan turned and saw the siblings on the floor, kneeling, with Ursula cradling her brother's bowed head.

"I was never his, do you know that?" Jonathan asked into her lap.

"You have my father as your own," she whispered fiercely. "He would have loved you."

Chapter 26

Winter 1862-63

Fenwick Pines Plantation, Maryland

All the outside plantings had been carefully bedded down for the winter, but the trees inside the Orangerie were green and vibrant inside the high windowed brick building set off from the plantation house. The lemon tree was even bearing fruit in winter. The fireplace's large stove kept everything warm. Rowan found them, Ursula's brother and his sister, with their heads together again. Rowan did not like the sound of her voice.

"Leave him to me."

Her usual low tones suddenly shot up higher at the sight of him in the arched doorway. "Ah, petit choux, the person we have been looking for! Come in, make yourself warm."

Huddled together on the bench, neither Jonathan's habitual slouch nor Marie Madeline's deft fingers mending a frilly cap showed signs of an intent of looking for anyone.

Jonathan smile twitched as he stood. "Yes, well, I had best be about showing Blake's men where the battalion might store supplies, shall I?"

Marie Madeline gave him one of her brook-no-nonsense smiles. "I think not. You will kindly feed the fire. Rowan, close the door, were you raised in a barn?"

Jonathan growled, scraping away a line of dirt from his forehead before he grabbed at the neatly piled stack of wood. He was a different, more purposed man here at his homestead, in more workmanlike clothes, tending the carefully cultivated lemon and orange trees, climbing up on roofs of slave cabins to repair leaks. Right now he looked like he'd rather be on one of those roofs.

"Well, then? Tell him," Marie Madeline demanded once he had fed the stove.

"The federal men, they refuse to recognize Ursula as your wife."

"Why?"

"They do not like the look of the marriage document. They suspect it may be fraudulent."

"It is fraudulent, Jonathan," Ursula said quietly, appearing from the other side of the central chimney.

Where had she come from? Rowan did not even feel a draft. How had she appeared? He glanced at the high French style doors at the entrance of the Orangerie. Still closed, their glass gleaming in the late afternoon sun. But there was another door at the far end. There were at least two ways into every building, no matter how small, at Fenwick Pines. One for servants, one for masters. Ursula knew them all, in this place full of secrets, where she moved in the silent glide Rowan knew from the battlefield and hospitals of his recovery. But here at the place of her birth, her movements were without substance, ghostlike, and set him on edge. She wore a shawl embroidered with flowers over a blue gown. Was the shawl warm enough? The gown was not the one his sister had provided her, except for Marie Madeline's fancy tatted lace collar at the neck. Was it Ursula's own, the summer sky gown, stored here since she was a girl? Was it her mother's? He stood, giving her his place by the stove's warmth.

"Ah, my darling Ursula, join us," Marie Madeline said for him, what he wanted to say, if he was not helplessly tongue-tied here, in this beautiful, fragrant part of her world.

Marie Madeline patted Rowan's surrendered place on the bench beside her brother. Ursula sat in a strange, artificial way, because of what was under the gown: hoops, like the ladies of Montreal and New York and Washington wore.

Johnathan glanced up at him. "Well, now this completes my family of judges and jury!" he proclaimed, peevish.

Ursula locked her gaze on her brother. "I did not sign that document," she said sternly.

"Yes, well, in the letter of the law, perhaps."

"Not perhaps."

He straightened his slouch. "But not the spirit!" He looked to Rowan. "Why is it so difficult to convince you both?"

Marie Madeline's brows shot up. "Both? Jonathan, you told me that Rowan signed!"

"He did! Although, well, he might have trouble remembering the exact nature of his engagement with this document. And I might have failed to tell him what required that damned scrawl."

Ursula shook her head. A few golden brown curls escaped her hair's shell comb. "Rowan has a fine writing hand. I should have guessed."

"Well, that is the reason we must do something official, in front of witnesses," Jonathan proclaimed.

The curl bounced against her cheek. Rowan fingers ached for the feel of her hair, and that cheek. "Our sergeant is a man of his word," she pronounced quietly, as if he were not there at all. "If we formalized this document with action, he will feel well and truly obligated. He will have no release from our entanglement, no future except one tied to me."

Jonathan grabbed her hand. "Tied to? Entanglement? What are you saying? The man loves you! Tell her, you idiot!"

"I do. Yes, of course I do, Sula." Rowan gave away his intimate name for her to her brother, to his Marie Madeline, to convince her.

It did not. Ursula's jaw tightened, her face flushed red. But she saved her rage for her brother as they continued to argue as if both he and Marie Madeline were not there.

"Loves me? After all we have put him through, why?" she demanded with quiet intensity.

"How should I know? But he lives to make you laugh, can you not see it? From the first, from that damned battlefield when he was willing to fry you a rat!"

Marie Madeline glanced up at Rowan, frowning. "What is this then? Another woman for whom you are frying rats? I thought I alone held that privilege."

Ursula pressed her brother's arm and continued their argument. "That was another time, a desperate time," she insisted, "Before he knew everything else."

"Husbands and wives are not supposed to know everything. That is what marriage is for, is it not, Madame Picard?"

Marie Madeline considered before nodding. "That was the way of it for me. With Olivier and Francois both. Though less so with Pierre, the first, who was a very simple man with very little mystery about him. Shooting birds and raising hell, that one. Still, he knew how to keep my back from the cold."

Jonathan laughed. "You see, sister? You and that great Irish addle brain will have years of peeling back the layers until you both despise each other."

Marie Madeline let out a laugh. "Now then, young sir. I despised none of them. I am a woman of taste in my men!"

"Jonathan, Madame Picard, stop." Ursula pleaded, her hand reaching for her mouth, her breaths straining at her corseted middle.

"Stop making you smile?" Jonathan challenged. "I am as helpless as your sergeant is against the power of that smile, sister dear. Will you not look at that poor besotted oaf? Will you not talk to him?"

"There is no need," Marie Madeline's voice rang out, arresting all their attention as when her fiddle announced the next dance. "It is I who will now have words with my brother."

She rose in all her bird of prey fury, and strode to his side.

"Rowan, I will not take this woman of yours under my roof until you marry her before a priest."

"But—"

"No objection will move me." She faced Ursula next. "And you, my darling, from you I will brook no more objections. For you have acquired a good and true man, who my sisters and I and his former amours have made ready for you. You could do many times worse for yourself."

Jonathan rose to his full height to face the taller woman. "A church wedding, Madame? My best horse those two have already cost me. And now a church wedding besides?"

Chapter 27

December, 1862

Ursula was grateful for the late season not yet bringing a hard frost. Miriam found pale blue asters and golden rod still growing wild for her bouquet. Enough to hide her shaking hands here in the tiny seaside chapel that one of her great-grandfathers designed.

Jonathan had traveled into town to fetch Captain Kane. Ursula remembered how her parents loved the mysterious Lucius Kane, who had once sailed with her father in their three-masted Baltimore clipper ship around Cape of Good Hope. The captain's adventures took him in and out of her life after her father's death. His visits were always joyous occasions, full of celebration and story.

She had first introduced him to Jonathan with, "Captain Kane! This is my brother. He has just turned three, you must teach him to swim!" Everyone thought her ten-year old self amusing. Except for Captain Kane, who took them to the cove the next morning and eased her concern for her water-loving brother's survival.

The young cleric Captain Kane brought to officiate was the gift of Doctor Cole in Washington. He was the medical company's chaplain, but had been the parish priest of his home town in the Hudson Valley of New York State, ministering to the iron workers at his mother's foundry. He was of middle years, and from Ireland, like Rowan. The merry twinkle in his eye made Ursula wonder if the captain doctor had sent a real priest. Father Healy had dispensed with banns as well as instruction considering she had been raised under the watchful eyes of nuns and Rowan the formidable Quebecois sisters. That was supposed to have given them enough sense to know what they were doing. Ursula understood what they were doing. Rowan was keeping her from imprisonment. She was ensuring her estate and its people continued in Jonathan's capable hands over her exile. This was a transaction without love at its center.

The church rang with Marie Madeline's fiddle playing one of Handel's more impatient Water Music suites full of allegro and andante.

Jonathan took her arm.

Their witnesses included Lucius Kane, the considerate and commanding Colonel Blake and his fellow officers who currently occupied the main house. Miriam had made sure they were all fresh pressed and formal. But she could do little to make Rowan look any more exotically dashing as the Zouave's dress uniform, which changed fighting blue to red pantaloons. Even with his beautiful glass eye replacing his patch, he still resembled an Irish pirate come to whisk her away as he stood at the small altar beside the great whirlwind of beautiful music that was his sister.

Father Healy had not objected to Miriam and Alfred inside the chapel among the guests, sitting in the last row and behind a wooden column. If Ursula did not have their smiles, their nods, and Madame Picard's beautiful lace collar gift, she was not sure she could have allowed Jonathan to propel her up the aisle.

Chapter 28

Her lips, so warm and moist and pliant when they had loved each other, trembled as they had pledged their troth with a public kiss. And her head remained bowed since the church ceremony, as if she were being led to the gallows, and not into her new life as his wife. But Ursula allowed Rowan to take her hand, here in the oldest, colony-times rooms of the mansion house. Portraits of her male ancestors and one forbidding female who reminded him of Marie Madeline looked down at him from the mahogany paneled walls. Him, the Irish usurper. Rowan's continuing sense of unease was turning to dread.

He wanted none of this. He only wanted her, his great protector bear. He wanted to show her that he loved her beyond measure, that he could keep her safe.

The lawyer shifted his papers, then turned in Rowan's direction.

"Mrs. Buckley has a life estate in the real property at Fenwick Pines, sir."

"What does that mean?" Rowan asked.

"That it will continue in the family. Her line."

Ursula lifted her head. She faced the lawyer. "Our people," she said, "What will become of them, when I leave here?"

"Why, that is for you to say, Mrs. Buckley. Maryland is a border state. It remains unaffected by the president's Proclamation Ninety-five."

Rowan flinched to hear it put so boldly. His wife owned human beings, even after Lincoln had freed those of the rebel states. This was not his America, the shining beacon of liberty.

"And may I remind you and your husband that the Maryland General Assembly has outlawed manumission by deed or will since the year 1860?" the lawyer said quietly.

Ursula's lemon balm scent intensified. "There is no need to remind us. I have been in communication with my brother on the legal status of our people over the past few years."

"Then you know that your people are your property. You are free to sell them, but forbidden to free them."

"I know the law as it currently stands."

His wife was so much more used to this world, Rowan realized. She rose from her chair. The men followed. "I believe I have all the counsel I require, thank you, sir."

She squeezed Rowan's hand and then finally raised her eyes to his.

"I am now prepared to speak with Colonel Blake and your superiors, Lieutenant Buckley," she said softly.

* * *

Later, she sat beside him at the wedding meal table, graciously receiving her guests, including families of neighboring plantations, smiling faintly at their remembrances of half her lifetime ago. Rowan took the measure of all the men about her own age. Did any give her added attention? Did any give him a look that said, "I have had your woman?" Rowan was ashamed of these thoughts, but he could not banish them. Was it the silk merchant, now with his rose-scented wife and two little ones who clambered up on Rowan's knee to examine his penny whistle? That made Ursula smile, deepening his shame over the pictures of his imagination: of his new wife and the silk merchant stealing away. When? On one of her visits home from the convent school? Stop it. Ursula showed the man no special attention. Nor did she give the neighboring plantation owners any extra courtesy. Most

145

were surely regarding him as the invading usurper of their land and way of life, but they were all formally solicitous.

The only man besides her brother to whom she showed outward affection was her father's friend, the ship's captain, Lucius Kane. Kane was wary of him. Rowan felt his steely eyes' assessment throughout the meal. Was he her first lover? It was possible, of course, but the affection they shared seemed much more like that of a doting uncle and his niece.

No, it must have been one of the younger swains, here or detained by the war, most likely on the Confederate side. Whoever it was, that one was so inept that Ursula thought lovemaking an occasion of pain. Rowan would like to throttle the man for mistreating her. And if Ursula ever chose to reveal the identity of the first man who claimed her heart, he resolved to do so.

Marie Madeline struck up a wedding dance on her fiddle. Alfred's banjo joined in a joyous rhythm. Then Captain Kane joined them with a sailor's button accordion. With the encouragement of her guests' stomping feet, his bride granted him a shy smile and tapped the penny whistle pocket Marie Madeline had sewn into his vest.

"Will you play too?" she asked softly.

His heart swelled. All past lovers were forgotten. There, then. How could he think of anything but pleasing her? He took his place beside the musicians.

Ursula rose. Her blue gown was embedded with satin ribbons that glowed in the candles' light. Colonel Blake, a courtly man with greying side whiskers bowed before her and asked for her to lead the lined reel that was forming. She took his gloved hands in hers and the dancers were off. Rowan watched the configurations, always keeping Ursula in his sight as she changed partners, bowed, spun.

The union officers took turns with his bride, then left cash payment at Marie Madeline's feet. Good God, Rowan thought, what was she up to? She'd explained the French Canadian wedding custom to them, no doubt. She leaned over to him.

"Stop scowling, petit frère. You think this place will run on good will when we are gone? They can spare the greenbacks."

The planters and their sons then took a dance turn with his bride. Rowan played on, watching Ursula, catching tunes from Marie Madeline, from Alfred and Captain Kane. Well, it was for the best. Even if his balance was what it had been before he lost the eye, he was not sure he could have followed the configurations his wife was pacing through with her partners. Hers were different than the country dances at home. More stately and English, even coming out of Alfred's lively, ringing instrument.

Finally Marie Madeline struck up a waltz, his bridegroom signal. At last, it was his turn. He returned his penny whistle in his vest's pocket and approached his bride. Her cheeks were flushed with pleasure and he caught a glimpse of the girl she once was, here in this room, dancing with all her admirers.

He took her waist, hoping Marie Madeline would keep the pace slow so he would not feel the oaf he was next to Ursula's delicate beauty. Soon he was bathing in her smile, for she followed his steps as if they had been dancing all their lives.

Chapter 29

The root cellar outside the summer kitchen was smaller than Ursula remembered. Its fragrant hanging hams were fewer than she remembered at this time of year. Deeper. She must go deeper, past the crates of apples, the jars of peaches and quince and pears. She used to love it here, playing hide-and-go-seek and where's-the-button with Jonathan, then learning household duties while strolling the aisles in a white apron that matched her mother's. In that time before everything went hard, cold, and lonely.

And then, on the night before they were to send her away with a husband, she'd hidden here. A poor choice. She had misjudged the depth of her stepfather's anger at her public refusal.

He came at her from behind, in the dark. He extinguished her light, and carried none of his own. And he had closed the door, leaving not even the moon or stars for guidance back into the beautiful night. He called her names she did not even understand until later. Jezebel. Harlot. Temptress. Seducer. He grabbed her hair, so carefully put up to look like she was not a high spirited girl who still played with her dolls, but a matron, like her mother. She still heard the pinging sounds of the hairpins on the wine bottles. She had groped, found a glass neck, swung hard. Missed. Broke it against the rack, not him, not his skull, where it should have landed.

He had her then.

The strap he'd brought to beat her with went around her neck. She could not speak, she could hardly breathe as he pressed her against the root cellar wall, yanked her arm behind her back until she thought it would break, shoved up her skirts, and entered her from behind. Again, again, until she thought she would break in two.

And then he released her and she collapsed, heaving, finding her breath in a sea of bubbling wine, broken glass, and her blood. He grabbed her hair one last time, snapping her head back.

"There. See what your defiance has made me do? Now you are ruined." And then the warning, in a voice soft, almost sounding surprised. At himself. Over what he had done. Over what he was about to say. "If you tell anyone, I will kill your mother and marry you myself. You will have a lifetime of this. Now clean yourself up. You will marry my dolt of a cousin as planned."

And then he was gone, leaving the door open, so that she could see the quarter moon's light, the stars again. Great, heaving sobs erupted from her mouth, past her shaking fingers. Bringing Sling, with his lantern, his always kind eyes.

"Miss Ursula? Oh, no, not you," his voice, only recently gone to a deep, man's tone cried, full of sorrow. Then his coat, over her shoulders, covering her ripped yellow party gown.

His coat had covered her shoulders once before, when the squall had come up as she and Jonathan and Sling fished together off Ratchitt's Bay.

"I am cold too!" Jonathan had complained, then.

"But we must take care of Miss Ursula first, young one," Sling told her brother, barely seven years old. "You always needs look after the womenfolk, hear, Master Jon?"

That memory, and Jonathan's wide-eyed nodding, was helping her breathe through the remembered anguish now. Fresh tears flowed freely, for that long-ago girl, whose life was about to turn.

It still smelled of wine and blood here, both metallic, both making her teeth ache. Why had she cried loud enough to bring over the engagement party guests?

"I sent him to you." The soft voice, his mother Miriam's, answered now. "It was usually one of his sisters, caught here, fetching onions or a jar of quince. That's why I sent my boy down here that night, Miss Ursula. To comfort one of his sisters."

"How did you know?"

"The Master, he had a look about him, each time, after. Crazed look. Never showed it to your mama, but we backstairs folk saw. Oh, child, angry as he was that night, we never thought he'd use you that way."

"The way he used your daughters."

"Well, yes."

"Sling left me his coat. Evidence, they said."

Miriam frowned. "Yep. Never had a lick of common sense as a boy, that one."

As a boy. As if Sling had been allowed to grow into his full manhood. As if his mother was still scolding him. As if Ursula and the best friend of her childhood had continued to age together. It was more than she could bear.

"Oh, Miriam. I am so sorry," the woman Ursula was now finally told her.

"Miss, you got nothing to be sorry about. That's why you went all quiet on us, in truth? That man tried to make you put the blame of it on Sling, on account of my child's coat, and his lantern left there?"

Ursula nodded, cast back into the silence again.

"And you never did, you never gave him up or bore false witness against our Sling. I won't never forget that. A fierce spirit in your eyes every time they ask you, back then. Every time you shook your head no, I was glad I helped your mama raise you up."

"They did not believe me."

"No. But you did not slander my child, your friend. I think the seed was planted in your mama then, that evil lived in her house."

"It made no difference."

"Sure it did. Cast some doubt amongst the slave catchers, even Old Man Munson and his bloodhounds, who never knew my Sling to disrespect a woman, black, brown or white."

"Doubt."

"A step. Munson, he never hired his bloodhounds out to the slave catchers after that night, did you know?"

"I did not. There is still so much I do not know. My stepfather, he told me…in front of the sisters at the convent, he told me how they hunted for Sling, how they, they…"

Miriam folded her in her arms, patted her back, as if Ursula had been the one who had lost a child. Which, of course, she had. Did Miriam know? Of her own child? The one who lived long enough to save her mother's life, to keep her away from him, protected among the nuns? Ursula had been able to see only a glimpse: a tiny, perfect foot, the limp fingers, before they'd taken her away. Then the angry shout from beyond the door. "White! The child was white, sir!" hurled by Sister Raphaela at her stepfather.

"Now, now, that times's gone, all gone," Miriam murmured.

Were Sling and her daughter who had not lived long enough to be granted even a name, or a headstone, were they with God now? There, in God's heaven, did He make her baby move, breathe, thrive? Did God find Sling's tongue, his hand, his man parts and put him back together, so he could be whole again, and teach her daughter to fish?

Miriam squeezed her hands. "Listen to me now, child. I got another story for you tonight. Your daddy, that fine gentleman and friend of our Captain Kane's, he thought to sail us away."

"Away?"

"Captain Kane did it too, with a few, the ones with deep longing in their eyes, who stared off the shore, stared to the east like their hearts would burst. He took them on as sailors for his clipper ship. They hunted the slavers, breaking the law, still bringing the captured to our shores. Then he brought some of those sailors home, to one of them African free colonies. Did you know that?"

Ursula shook her head.

"Caused a row or two with your mama, I'll say. 'Stealing my people,' she called it, until your daddy, he brought her closer towards his and the captain's way of thinking. About who was who among people stealers. Well, we most of us ain't goin' back to Africa, Miss Ursula. This our home. When the fightin' of this war's done we still going to be together, black and white, here in America. We best slow down them bloodhounds and consider each other more like fellow children of God." She helped Ursula to her feet. "Let's go away from this place now. There be too many haunts for us both."

Chapter 30

Miriam fell a step behind her as they walked. "You not dressed in no God's woman clothes no more, Miss Ursula. You got a fine Yankee soldier husband now, waiting for you at your marriage bed. That mean Jubilo approaches?"

"My hope is that you will all belong to only yourselves soon."

Miriam tilted her head. "Soldiers of both sides come and go in this part of Mary's land."

"Yes. But no more of the grays, not here at Fenwick Pines, not with all these federal soldiers stationed here."

"Too many! We'd best get some of the fine old furniture in the attic, Miss Ursula! They so big and clumsy, them Yankee soldiers!"

"Good idea."

She stopped and looked deeply into Miriam's eyes. "The federals, they think I have helped the other side. They suspect Jonathan as well."

"You two? They soft-headed, them Yankees?"

Ursula smiled, remembering their conspiracies here in the borderland, and so close to the sea. Of visiting slaves from other plantations, who would walk along the shore, the swamps, then disappear. And before that, she knew now, her father and Captain Kane, somehow spiriting some to free colonies in Africa. How in the world had they done that?

"I will be leaving. I have leased Fenwick Pines to the Yankee generals for the duration of the war. And when the battles begin again, I expect they will need it as a hospital."

"Your brother, will he stay?"

"I hope he will. He has run the place well?"

"Miss Ursula, your mama did right to trust him to the task until you came into your rights to it this day. He took on after your mama's ways, that one. For all his sass, he be a good man." Miriam frowned. "Sent none of us down Georgia way, even in bad years. He learned them farming ways from the science men, from our own people as he walked the tired tobacco fields. Changed them all over. And did not take to the gambling and catting around, no Miss! Only the horses. Oh he does love the horses, starting with the ones your mama left to him, to be sure. But not the betting on them, no, Miss! So there was no need, you see, to sell any of us folk off, because he could breed and train a good horse, instead of us. There ain't been debt since he been overseeing the place. We are all together still. Excepting you, child. This your home, and you be leaving? We just now welcomed you back."

"And a grand welcome. But I cannot remain. Because of their suspicions. For now, I ask our people to stay and provide. Some of the federals will work beside you on the farm."

"White men, aside from Master Jon? In the fields?"

"Yes. They are a different sort than we are used to. The army men have sworn to treat you all decently, and they have been men of their word. But it seems Mr. Lincoln has emancipated all but those in the border states. To keep those states in the union, you see?" Ursula couldn't look Miriam in the eyes. She had failed her for so long.

But she felt a strong hand rest on her shoulder.

"We are used to them men in Washington and their unholy compromises. Don't you be fretting too much on it. Ain't you done any of it."

"If the men wish to work for the army stationed here, I'm afraid their wages will be paid to my brother, as my agent. But we have spoken on these things. Jonathan will then give all the money to the worker and his family. It is the best I can do, for now. Until the war has ended, and perhaps I am permitted to return."

"Where you goin' now? With your man?"

"No. I have caused him great trouble. He must stay at his duties. I go North."

"North?"

"To Canada."

"They banishing you from your own country, Miss Ursula?"

"They are. But I go to my husband's family. Good people."

Miriam touched her cheek, as she often did when Ursula was a child. The nuns were kind, but did not show signs of physical attention. Only Sister Raphaela ever squeezed Ursula's hands, touched her cheek in fondness.

"Well. I be comin' too."

Ursula's breath caught suddenly in her delight. "Of course you are welcome, in my employ. And Miriam, you will be free because there are no slaves in Canada."

"For long time gone, Miss, I know this about your man's homeland. From the ones who passed through, who still pass through, thanks to your brother turning his back, or even helping us launch a boat. But I know since my granddaddy joined up with them English in that second American war with them. That's when I first heard of Canada."

Ursula's astonishment must have shown, for the older woman laughed. "You got your books, Miss Ursula. But we got stories."

"Yes of course. It has been a long time since I have enjoyed your good company, Miriam. I have much to learn, and remember. I am so happy you will be my companion."

"Well, now. Companion, is it? I best learn the value of that myself, yes, Miss. For I hear tell you be a rich woman, by way of your Yankee daddy. I might need myself a new hat, you think?"

Ursula laughed. "If you will help me choose one for myself as well.'

Chapter 31

Rowan preferred the secrecy of their past assignations to the knowing grins of the soldiers, of the servants. Damnation. He was already thinking of them as what Ursula called them: servants, not slaves.

The one named Miriam, who despite her small size was the boss woman of the big house, had shown him the outside of the structure that she called the garden cottage when he'd first arrived. It was like no cottage Rowan had ever seen in his other homes, either the modest Quebecois timber structures with their sloping roofs, or the thatch and stone cabins of the tenant farmers of county Leitrim. This cottage was the size of a small barn or storehouse. And balanced in design, looking more like a Grecian temple with its flat board painted siding, its four front columns and triple hung windows.

Miriam and the frock coat-wearing Alfred met him there at dusk. The two had left the celebration of the wedding early to work together inside the cottage. Dust and spider web remnants still clung to them, but excitement shone in their eyes before Miriam left to fetch her mistress.

"This be more quiet, more comfortable for the two of you, Lieutenant, sir, with all the bustlin' still going on yonder," Alfred had assured him kindly. The kindnesses surprised Rowan. And none of the slaves he had met at Fenwick Pines wore fear or fury in their expressions or movements, or at least hid it well. He was used to the desperate, grim determination runaways that the army called contrabands, as if they were discarded rifles or unmanned horses after a battle.

Now, as night was descending and his social duties at the big house ended, Rowan followed Alfred past the double wooden doors and inside the garden cottage. The servant carried a globed astral oil lamp, casting its halo of light.

The scent came first: of linseed oil, mixed with the earthy smells of a creek bed, strong herbals, and books. The books lining the high, wide desk appeared. Alfred raised the lamp so Rowan could scan the titles. The Last of the Mohicans, Two Years Before the Mast, Gulliver's Travels. He touched the leather spines.

"You be seeing it all better tomorrow, sir, with the north light shining through them high windows the day long," Alfred explained. "The captain, he did love his artist light."

"Captain?"

"Miss Ursula's daddy, sir. Captain Martin was his name. He had himself a clipper ship, and was friend to Captain Kane. He helped us build our garden cottage, of his own style notions. Weren't nothing like it at the Pines before him, no sir! So you see he departed young, but left his mark in design and daughter both."

Alfred rested his free hand's fingers in his trousers' braces. "We sure enough did not think it would stand, not with all the great barn door size holes we put in the place for windows! But Captain Martin, he been to them old places like Rome and the Greek islands, and he said for us not to worry none. And he needed the light, you see, for his making of these here."

Rowan turned his head toward where the old man next brought the lamp--the wall without windows. It was full of paintings: large, glorious paintings, of ships, of the sea in every weather, from squall to storm to fine.

"That was his home before he came to us, you see, sir, the waterways. Now most of us folk, we hated that big water, hatred passed on from the old ones, and their passage into bondage. But Captain Martin, he said passage goes in all directions on the mighty Atlantic. East. South. Even north. And proved it too, at great danger to himself."

"How? How did he prove it?"

"I best let our mistress, or young Master Jon talk to you on that, sir, when they ready. It still be dangerous here on the borderlands, sir."

The swirling scents of the room circled them. "He painted here, Ursula's father?" Rowan asked, now feeling fully as awed as the first time the Maries brought him inside the doors of Montreal's Notre Dame Cathedral. The same yearning filled him now: to meet the ones who had achieved such beauty.

"He did, sir, and was musical too, playing that squeezebox there on the stool, see? How we all laughed together in them times."

"Before Mrs. Kingsley's second marriage. To Jonathan's father."

The man's eyes narrowed. "Person can't help who his daddy is, sir. We know that here in the Southland," he said quietly.

Of what was he being accused Rowan wondered? Misjudgment of the current steward of Fenwick Pines, Ursula's brother? Yes. And something more. Deeper, more personal, but Rowan could not shake it out among all the strangeness of this place, this life of his wife's family.

Alfred moved further into the room with the lamp. "Captain Martin, he studied the rocks and the plants. A learned man with a kind heart, a heart like our Miss Ursula's. Why, we could not get either one to stay out of our kitchens when a bit of mint or angelica took their fancy!"

"She has kept up her studies," Rowan said. "She is a good healer."

"She says the same of you, sir. That you are a man full of grace and mercy and healing power."

"I am a broken down soldier, Alfred. Nothing more."

"Well. If'n you say so, sir."

Rowan scanned past the boxed collections of mosaic fragments, and the carved classical busts, to the glass case containing arrowheads. At last, things he knew. The arrowheads looked like the ones he often found while plowing the Maries' fields at home, relics of the Indian wars.

Alfred placed the lamp in the middle of a small round table covered with a red silk cloth. It was set out with a savory pie, cakes, and a steaming pot of tea.

"Thank you, Alfred. For this. For your fine playing at the banjo."

"It gave me pleasure to join in. You and Madame Picard both got yourselves some tuneful ways. Miss Ursula, she told us you be musical, like her daddy."

"Did she?"

"She did."

He turned. It was not the servant's voice this time, but Ursula's. She stood beside the smiling Miriam, who lifted Ursula's roses-woven shawl higher around her mistress's shoulders before both she and Alfred backed away.

Ursula touched his hand. "They were afraid of you at first, you see, Rowan. Imagine that? I did not wish for them to be afraid. So I told them stories. Of you, of us."

"Are we together so long and well as to merit stories now, wife?" he teased her.

She smiled in that rueful way he loved.

The glowing lamplight cast her and the soft creamy whites of her clothing in its radiance. And then the creak of the doors' hinges and the servants were gone. The room held only the two of them, and the linseed scent.

There was Ursula, beautiful, beside the bed. He approached. Her hair was held back with a blue ribbon. Her fingers began working at the buttons of his uniform coat.

Ursula, his wife, breathed against the skin of his neck, his chest.

"They have left us supper," he said.

The shawl fell to the floor, the blue ribbon sifting through his fingers, following.

"Yes. Later."

"Oh, my darling girl. We will be well and truly wed, if this is what you desire."

"It is what I desire." Her fingers stilled, suddenly. Her voice became a hushed whisper. "And you? Rowan, my sheltering tree, are you sure of us?"

"As sure as the moon."

"The moon is sometimes dark."

"Not dark. New."

He took her small waist between his hands. No stays, not corseted. And no hoops. Thank you, Miriam. Shoulders, bare now, without their roses shawl. He could keep his wife, his Ursa Major, warmer than her beautiful adornments.

How could he face new moon nights, months, years without her? You great idiot. She will be safe with the Maries, while you find who has slandered her. She may be a slaveholder, but she was no traitor to America's unity.

Later, these tasks.

There is only now, her arms, the feel of her tongue, swiping across the tuff of beard he'd managed to grow back under his chin. For her. How was it that she loved that, loved him at all? How did Ursula say he was like her father, that accomplished man, who knew the sea, who made such beautiful paintings?

He only knew how to kill. And now he was scarred, ugly, because of it. Stop. Stop thinking, when her touch was so...

"Rowan?"

He lifted his head from between lush, full breasts, more full than he remembered from their first time together among the peach trees. To her eyes and their habitual sadness that broke his heart.

"Aye, love?"

"We must remember this."

"Oh, aye."

Chapter 32

Abda was as small as a child and usually given this task, of finding out what was said beyond the house, beyond the close-by grounds. The worst things were talked about there. She knew how to disappear in the woods, the darkest of all the places she was sent. Miriam had taught her well, how to be the eyes and ears of the folk of Fenwick Pines.

So she followed the two fine-suited gentlemen, the ones even the most full-of-gold-stars army men listened to. Abda worried that even her well-honed senses could not decipher the clicks and speed of their Yankee talk. But she had deer ears, Miriam said. Abda slipped close, behind a pine whose trunk was almost as thin as she.

"It has been decided. We will not have another Mrs. Greenhow on our hands. Our intelligence service has been made the laughing stock of the damned English, French and the world around. Not again. The woman will not reach her destination."

"But—"

"No international incidents, of course. Keep that Canadian woman of his here."

"How?"

"Call her a hostage, a safeguard, until the new Mrs. Buckley is over the border. Except that there will be an unfortunate accident before she arrives at the border. Condolences to the family, send Madame Picard home, and it is finished. We have plenty of people on the rail lines.

They can do it clean, neat. It is a long journey. They should wait for when the time is right."

"She will not be alone. She will have that servant with her."

"The negro housekeeper, yes. That brother of hers presides over a different kind of these people: not bowing, heads down, respectful. They look you in the eye, these. It is…unsettling. They cannot be counted upon to be intimidated. So Mrs. Buckley's lady's maid will die, too. She will no doubt try to save her mistress, yes? She will fall onto the tracks too. We must make sure. It will be worth the cost."

"Cost, sir?"

"A bit of propaganda for the land of magnolias and happy, self-sacrificing slaves. That is, if the little black spaniel is mentioned at all in the public accounts."

Chapter 33

"Ain't getting on any train, Miss Ursula."

"But, that is the way they have decided we will travel."

"And I ain't your black dog, no, Miss!"

"Miriam, please tell me what has you so distressed."

"You got to do your own decidin' now, Miss. Ain't sayin' your man is bad, nor the army men, neither. But there be others."

"Others?"

Miriam cracked open the lowest of the cottage window's inside shutters. "The high hat men with the snake eyes. Out there, talking with your man now, see them? They no good for you. For me neither. Will you listen about what Abda heard last night in the woods, Mistress?"

Ursula felt the cold ride up her arms and pulled her mother's shawl closer. "Yes. I am listening."

Miriam told her the rest as Ursula watched Rowan, his hands behind his back, among the government men, the ones in black civilian clothes. They did not resemble the army officers, who were more like Rowan, with broad honest faces and good manners, men who were made hard and beaten down by this war, but who had other lives, as storekeepers and farmers and scholars, lives they longed to return to, just as Rowan longed for his life in Canada with his beautiful sisters. The black-suited men held no rank, with not even a mister attached to their names when they spoke to her, to each other. And, now, to him. Rowan's fine officer's coat was misbuttoned, his wild curls uncombed because he'd dressed in such haste after the disturbance of their early morning lovemaking.

Miriam whispered behind her. "I know he be your husband, Miss Ursula. But you cannot obey Lieutenant Buckley. Maybe he means to save you, in this deal he done made with them. To go to his sisters, live in his Canada home. Look at them, Miss. Look hard. Their eyes always on their boots, not on your man. White men don't be acting that way with each other, unless they lying. We will not be safe, even if we can get there without falling on them railroad tracks, like they plan for us. Even if we get north, they will find us among your man's Canada folk. And they will finish our time on this earth."

Ursula's thoughts scattered. She turned from the window, rested her hand on her servant's shoulder.

Suddenly, the older woman grinned, showing off the gold tooth Ursula's father had provided after the Christmas bonfire accident.

"Miss. You believe me."

Ursula focused on those determined dark eyes. "Of course I believe you."

"Well, then. Your Miriam and her Uncle Alfred got things fixed. They will tell Captain Kane. He standing by, since we sent word out to him that you be comin' home from your time with the nuns, you see? We will make ready."

"Captain Kane?"

"Sure enough. He don't travel the seven seas no more. He been on coastal duties. And you think your daddy's friend ain't been keepin' up with your doings here? He smells a rat, too. We make a new plan with him, with his fleet little ship, for our passage north. We knows some few things about safe passage, the captain and us, you see. He get us out on the next tide, if you be willin.'"

"I--" Ursula's breath caught in her throat. Things were moving so swiftly. She watched Rowan's hands tighten there, behind his back, as he nodded, then took his leave of the men who wanted her dead. Who wanted her dear Miriam dead?

Lieutenant Rowan Buckley, her young husband, full of kindness and compassion. Bound to her in a new marriage.

Agreed to when he was ill and confused, by way of her brother's tricks. Without knowing who she was. There were so many secrets left, swirling with them in the dark as they gave each other pleasure. How could she think that they could have a love like her parents had? Why had she now bound herself to him truly, with ties that only death could unlatch?

What would her beloved man think when he found them gone?

Ursula realized that she had to risk even Rowen's hatred. Because she owed Miriam too much not to make this leap into the unknown. And for their child, hers and Rowan's, who deserved a better chance at life than her first-born.

"I am willing," she said.

Chapter 34

The courtyard-like entrance room of the main house rang out with quick paced footsteps on its oil floor cloth, painted in a trompe l'oeil cube design. All the searchers carried the same message: the mistress of Fenwick Pines and her maidservant had disappeared.

The government men's eyes narrowed. "She has outfoxed you both."

"Unless you have allowed, even engineered her escape."

"Escape? Escape?" Jonathan's fine nostrils flared in his indignation. "Mrs. Buckley, after two attempts on her life while she was in your nursing service, was being placed in her husband's family's care for safe-keeping! How dare you speak of an escape? She has suffered an abduction!"

"I would have slain any who attempted this!" Marie Madeline raged. "You brutes! You cowards!"

Jonathan strutted past the house servant Alfred and around the government men. Rowan tried to breathe as he grappled with his confusion, his grief. The heady scent of his bride had worked his way into his clothing, his hair, his ragged, uneven breathing. "We must remember this" she'd said, before he'd taken her down on their marriage bed again and again. She'd known she was leaving. Ursula had not trusted him. She had abandoned him.

Stop, Jonathan's eyes demanded even as his soft southern tones continued hurling vindictive at the government men. Can you not see the more immediate danger?

Yes. Deal with your broken heart later, petit frère, Marie Madeline's look also told him.

He could not. Grief threatened to engulf him as the argument echoed around the room.

"Abduction?" the government man spat back at them with quiet menace. "When her maid has disappeared along with her? The two of them, gone with this damned Maryland mist?"

"Two helpless women? Are you mad? They have been taken, I say! And you offer our servant Miriam's uncle, standing right before you, no consolation upon the loss of his niece, along with the woman they have both doted upon since childhood?"

"Such barbarity!" Marie Madeline agreed.

The government man stood toe to toe with her. "We are at war, sir, madame! And a suspected agent of the Southern cause has gone missing! Do you think I have time to worry about the sensibilities of a darkie footman?"

"As you are fighting to end the forced servitude of Alfred and all his fellow Americans, oui, monsieur, I expect that, exactly!"

Alfred's white-gloved hand reached to cover his face as both Jonathan and Marie-Madeline approached him. "You have my own consolation of the heart at least," Madame Picard offered.

"I am sure your dear one and Mrs. Buckley will provide strength over their travails." Jonathan added.

"Yes, sir, madame. Thank you, sir, madame. I expect they will look after each other. Lord willing, we all live for a reunion amongst us."

Jonathan, Marie-Madeline and the quick-witted servant kept up their bamboozle of the government men as Rowan fell further into his sorrow. He breathed in that lemon balm scent, still lingering from her hands raking through his scalp, her kisses pressed into his scars the night long.

Ursula was gone. By unknown and perhaps treasonous means, she had left him.

Chapter 35

January, 1863
Gardner Law Offices, Manhattan

Captain Kane's broad face, even with its hair and beard now greying, became the familiar one of her childhood, from his visits, before he was banished soon after he'd taught an adoring Jonathan to swim. Why? Was it for offering her mother, perhaps all three of them, the same escape, the same safe passage he had now provided to her and Miriam? In this loud tumultuous city of New York, his eyes squinted harder even than at sea. They became fierce.

"I am so glad you agreed to this, Mrs. Buckley," he said quietly as she turned from the carriage window's view of cobbled streets bursting with people. "You have given me a second chance."

"I am your Ursula, Captain Kane, not only on board the fine and fleet Vigilant, but always." Ursula struggled to keep her voice steady. Captain Kane had known how her own life had gone, thanks to Miriam, who was now setting their meager belongings into the hotel suite. "You continue to honor my family, sir. My father had a treasured friend in you. It is my fervent hope that my son or daughter will too."

His eyes widened. "Ursula. Are you sure?"

"Yes. More importantly, Miriam is sure. And Miriam is a gifted midwife."

"Ha!" he proclaimed now. "You had your father's stout gut on the water! Were never seasick as a child! I knew it was something else, but did not suspect something so, well, wonderful."

Over their Atlantic journey Lucius Kane provided more stories of a seafaring friendship since before Ursula was born. Her father and his dearest friend had served Britain and the United States, raiding slave ships that were determined to continue their unholy service after laws forbid it. Captain Kane was the bold face of their fleet, her father the more bookish, artistic and rational half of their team.

Uptown from the bustling docks of New York, the carriage brought them into her well-appointed lawyer's office. Captain Kane remained by her side, though she was sure he'd rather be off on his next shipboard adventure. Ursula thought of him, of Rowan, of her brother, and the Maries. How did she deserve such magnificent people in her life?

Except that those last were not. They could not be in her life now.

Stop this, she told herself while being seated in the room whose high walls were lines in bookcases. She had brave Miriam. And these two men. The one beside her, and the be-speckled Mr. Garner, sitting across the substantial desk.

Ursula had never questioned how her father had come into his fortune. She had lived most of her young life with her mother's people and inheritance. They had treated her father like Grace Calvert's peculiar indulgence— the English artist with no interest in anything but his family, the sea, and his paints, who carefully transcribed the notes of slave music, and never helped his neighbors recover runaways.

Now Henry Martin's own life, his earlier life, was laid out before Ursula by the ageless solicitor with the merry eyes and full white beard. He explained the extent of her father's holdings and how they'd been managed and increased in the years following his death.

Ursula touched the more personal document, her father's letter to her, lovingly preserved, like her memories of him. She felt again his arm over her shoulder as he read to her, his fingers guiding hers on how to hold a paint brush, lifting her among the branches, so she could smell the peach blossoms.

"Child of my heart" was how her father addressed her throughout the document. Ursula looked at the date. One month before her birth. He had not known her yet when he wrote this. And she was unaware that her laughing, bright-eyed father had this serious, haunted side.

There, laid out in his fine script was his own childhood. Born into English wealth and privilege, allowed the freedom of a third son to follow his heart, to indulge in his love of art and history and the natural world. And then came the seafaring, the travel, through his grandfather's merchant fleet. But eventually in his freewheeling, artistic life, his solid, ruled-by-convention family realized that dangerous ideas had taken hold. Ideas of friendship among the classes like that with Captain Kane, who introduced him to the evil that allowed one being to own another. Her father was then banished to America. Those ideas took more firm root in the soil of the South through his marriage to Grace Calvert.

To his English relatives, it was an advantageous match for a third son. He was finally coming around to his proper place in the world. But their world turned upside down when his older brothers met early, childless ends and he became the sole heir. That's when his association with Mr. Gardner and his New York law firm began. And when all the family's investments changed. Away from cotton, rum, and coffee. And into the city of New York in all its imperfect glory.

Ursula's fingers traced her father's signature, as they did together when she was a child on his knee. What he had bequeathed to her had almost been lost, dissolved into the vast wealth of the Catholic Church. No wonder there was talk of her leading her own motherhouse before she had even fully professed her vows. And there would be a generous arrangement towards increasing her stepfather's worth, no doubt. After all these years, was he going to settle for that?

"Since your father's will stipulates that you be over twenty-one years of age and married, or reach the age of thirty unwed, you have now come into your inheritance."

"My husband has no knowledge of this, Mr. Gardner."

"Nor has he any claim. In 1829, the laws degree that married women have control over their own inheritance, Mrs. Buckley, so I will abide by your instructions alone," Mr. Gardner informed her quietly, as he began opening documents, accounts, deeds.

Her place in this commerce-driven city was secure now, by way of two men: her father and the good man she had married, then abandoned.

Mr. Gardner's accounts of the holdings, yearly rents, and philanthropy continued, threatening to overwhelm her. But she was good with numbers, with accounts, Sister Cecelia had assured her at the motherhouse. She had gifts, useful gifts, from God.

Ursula lifted her head.

"I need to remain unknown, Mr. Gardner."

"You have come to the right city for that to be accomplished, Mrs. Buckley."

"Might I take on another name?"

"Whatever name you wish to give yourself. I shall draw up papers."

"Major, then."

"It shall be so, Mrs. Major."

Beside her, Captain Kane smiled. "You are almost a constellation."

"Almost," she said.

Chapter 36

Frederick, Maryland
January, 1863

Rowan watched Captain Merritt check the campfire clothesline's socks. The new men of Company D stood by, wide-eyed and confused as their commanding officer nodded curtly.

"They may proceed," Lieutenant," Merritt ordered.

"Go on, you wet-behind-the ears fresh fish."

"You heard Lieutenant Buckley!" Jonathan followed his nod. "Get those dry socks on your feet! Then you may read your mail."

The men were quick to obey his command, still eyeing the overflowing satchels.

Together with their captain, Rowan and Jonathan watched the recent recruits snatch up their knitted and darned footwear, white canvas gaiters and leather jamberees with the eagerness of children.

"Mind you do not singe your lady-wife's handiwork in your haste, Private Hayes," Jonathan admonished. "They will thank us when not blistered up from today's march, eh, kin?"

"I am your Lieutenant," Rowan reminded him.

His brother-in-law gave out a familiar snort. "And how you even remain in the army, I cannot fathom."

"That you were allowed in at all is what baffles me, Parlor Soldier," Rowan countered.

Jonathan carefully dusted his uniform's sleeve with its new sergeant's stripes. "Desperate times," he acknowledged cheerfully, with a wink at their captain.

Merritt shook his head. "Gentlemen, I expect both your present ranks stem from the fact that the army does not like to admit mistakes. Careful to transgress no more, or you will be commissioned as generals by week's end. Now, let us kindly dispense the mail."

Rowan knew his captain was right— throwing him out or an army demotion would reflect badly on the government agents themselves after Ursula and Miriam disappeared, as would continuing to keep Marie-Madeline as a hostage. So, while he was dumbstruck with grief, Jonathan went to work. He pressed Marie-Madeline into service as overseer of Fenwick Pines and proposed to join Rowan in military service. These outlandish displays of their loyalties only his brother-in-law could have engineered. To Rowan's astonishment, all was agreed to.

In addition, it was now easier for the government agents to keep track of them all.

Rowan hated being a commissioned officer, but he liked being back with his company, which was now widely known as Merritt's Zouaves. And he enjoyed mail times, calling names, emptying the treasured sacks, watching their new Pennsylvanian recruits share the packages of goods from home with the street-wise New Yorkers, most of them orphans, who had received nothing.

Once the mail bags were emptied, their captain invited them into his tent where they opened their own letters and packages together.

* * *

"Remember to keep your own socks dry, and your head down, now that you are a married man," Captain Merritt instructed, as he eyed Rowan's stack of opened letters from Canada and Fenwick Pines. "Any word?"

Rowan knew what his superior meant. Of Ursula. Of her safety. Had she and Miriam reached Canada?

"No, sir."

The captain returned to reading his mailed copies of four New York city newspapers. He always began with the New York Tribune, moved on to the Evening Post and New York Times, and finally Harper's Weekly.

Jonathan placed one of Marie-Madeline's raspberry jam tarts under Rowan's nose, as he addressed their superior. "Is New York City really infested with Copperhead rebel sympathizers, sir?" he asked.

Captain Merritt looked up from his perusal. "I'm afraid the Peace Democrats hold considerable sway still, yes, by all published accounts."

"How can that be?"

"Commerce, especially ties to the cotton trade."

"Several of my friends came south to work in the cotton mills of Massachusetts," Rowan remembered.

"They live and work among strangers?" his brother-in-law marveled.

"And, when excluded, they formed their own communities among them."

Captain Merritt smiled. "That's the story of my home on Manhattan island as well. Neighborhoods and pockets of Freemen, Irish, Germans, French, Dutch, Scandinavians, even a few Chinamen. New York is a city of strangers from all over the world."

Rowan nodded. "Never have I heard so many languages as when in your city, sir."

Captain Merritt laughed. "In good times they tolerate each other. Even become friends, intermarry, frightening the bigots with their grave warnings of amalgamation. But in times of strife they are often at each other's throats."

"I understand your learned knowledge, Captain," Jonathan declared, "you are a collage man. But how does this Canadian farmer know so much about our country?"

"We are side by side peoples, Canadians and Americans," Rowan maintained. "We share history and culture. We have Loyalists from your last revolution and many of your slaves as citizens, both, eh? And more land.

But in numbers of people, we are the mouse to your elephant. It is vital for us to know where you step."

"One of those strife times may be coming," Jonathan acknowledged, refolding the last letter of his stack. "Our seafaring friend Captain Kane says there is talk of our country following the South's example of last spring to increase forces."

"Starting a conscription policy?" Captain Merritt asked.

"Just so."

"Such speculation devours columns of Harper's, the Tribune and Herald too. There's talk of a lottery draft system before our third fighting season begins in earnest."

"Truly?" Rowan asked.

"As intrepid volunteers such as I are in short supply, no doubt," Jonathan claimed.

"The government would do much better to allow them in," Rowan groused, nodding to where Aaron and Silas, who were cooking up a fine stew an open fire for Company D. The two friends were ready to return in the rear of battle lines with their shovels to dig ditches and graves once the next battle began.

"Come the first of July, all slaves of the Confederacy will be emancipated. Units of black soldiers will start forming," their Captain informed them.

Jonathan sounded wistful. "I expect we will lose them."

"Oh yes, quite right."

Rowan considered Silas and Aaron's other federal service obligation. "Unless they are not let off the duty of keeping their eagle eyes on you."

"Me? I am serving the Union cause. You are the immigrant, married to a runaway suspect! Besides, how could we disappear?" Jonathan demanded. "We are in the middle of a rather conspicuous company, thanks to our peerless captain."

It was Merritt's turn to snort. "That is why we must train our new men well in Zouave tactics. They are such good targets for the sharpshooters."

"I'd hate to lose you, Captain Merritt," Jonathan conceded. "Even if you are a lawyer."

Rowan regarded his brother-in-law quietly. "You are doing right by the men," he said. "That should erase any remaining suspicions."

For once, Jonathan's smile was not edged with cynicism. "They will make good soldiers. And Aaron and Silas? I expect they already are."

Chapter 37

Gramercy Park, Manhattan
January 1863

On her first excursion with her property agent among her city holdings, Ursula stared up at the elegant row of town homes on Gramercy Park. Separate from the bustling streets of Manhattan Island surrounding it, she could finally breathe. The homes were tall and stately, each with its own grounds and carriage houses. But it was what they shared: the large, communal gardens in their midst, that drew her close, even as the gardens were now under a blanket of snow. The agent pointed out the four structures that she owned.

"Are any of these homes not presently occupied?"

"One, Ma'am. The tenant, a dry goods merchant named Thomas Selby, reported to us that the roof needs repairs. We arranged for Mr. Selby and his family to finish out his lease at one of your finer properties, one closer to his store. Rest assured, he did not complain at the prospect."

"Mr. Selby's home is presently vacant, then?"

"Yes, Mrs. Major."

"Might we look inside?"

"Of course, Ma'am."

Soon Ursula stood in the high kitchen, listening to the agent and Miriam's footsteps on the floor above. She wiped the mist from the windowpane and looked out past the high stoop and into the gardens. Two men strolled there, each holding a child's hand between them. The child broke away from them, and chased a squirrel until it disappeared into the high branches of an oak tree.

Her companions joined her.

"Do you like it here, Miriam?" she asked.

"It be quiet. I do, Miss Ursula."

"Good." She turned to the manager. "Do you think Mr. Selby and his household would be content to remain at the property nearer his place of business? At the same monthly rent, of course."

"I am sure they would be Ma'am, but the property is worth double the rent price."

"Good. That might make up for the trouble caused. Must keep roofs in good condition, sir. Please have them all checked yearly so we do not inconvenience another family."

He scribbled in his book. "Yes, Mrs. Major."

"Thank you. That is enough for today. Please send word to us at the hotel when repairs on the roof are complete. We shall live here."

"But, Ma'am, you have claim to much larger abodes, more well-appointed. This house is not in the most fashionable part of the island. It is a small village, really, and occupied at present by, well, not the finest class of people."

"Oh? And what class is that?"

He moved closer to her as if confiding a secret. "Actors and artists, most of them. Not suitable for the likes of such a lady of means as yourself."

"Might we move in a week's time?"

He sighed. "I will make sure all is ready."

Chapter 38

Ursula woke, as always, longing for Rowan's arms about her. How was that possible, when she'd lived so much more of her life without those arms?

Outside her bed chamber's windows, another gentle snow was falling, blanketing the gardens in white and sending a peaceful hush over the city. She heard scurrying, barely perceptible noises. She liked the town house's symmetry. If she stood at the top of either front or back stairwell, she would know from where the sound emanated. Ursula wrapped her flower shawl about her shoulders and stood at the top of the back stairs' landing. Soft voices. Excited, happy, coming from the kitchen. Miriam was awake before daylight, perhaps talking to a tradesman. Would they allow her to join them, to learn more about the running of a household, and to ease her loneliness?

Once she'd climbed down the two flights, Ursula opened the top of the Dutch door that separated the laundry room from the hearth-centered kitchen.

Before the stove was a man and two small children. The children's feet dangled in the air where they sat on the high-backed bench. The steaming scent of licorice came from the white teapot and cups on the table. Their backs were to her, but Ursula could tell they were engrossed in one of Miriam's handkerchief tricks. Miriam could turn a handkerchief into anything: a rabbit, a ghost, a trap for catching minnows in the stream. Now it was puffed up and tied off into the form of a small white mouse, and she was in the process of putting in the magic that would bring the creature to life.

"And what words do you know, young ones, to conjure some spirit into this here critter?" Miriam asked in her storyteller voice.

The smaller child pressed herself shyly into the man's side, but the older one tilted her head.

"Hoo doo?" she asked quietly.

"Oh, 'hoo doo' for sure!" Miriam approved, as she curled her fingers over the handkerchief mouse and put the magic in, "Hoo doo and ju ju both!" Miriam eased closer to the shy child. "You got something make this critter jump, little sister?" she asked.

The man's voice left a deep, soft rumble at the child's ear.

"Rotten tomatoes!" she proclaimed, after his prompt.

Miriam laughed and sprung her fingers into action with the spell. "Just so! Rotten tomatoes! That ought to do it!"

The mouse leapt from her hand then, and into the older child's lap. The girls laughed with glee. Ursula swung open the lower half of the kitchen door. The four turned, startled, and the spell was broken.

All stood. The man bowed, casting his handsome laughing face in shadow. The little girls both pressed into his side. They were beautiful, in matching blue checked pinafore dresses. Miriam stepped forward.

"We sorry to wake you, Miss Ursula."

"It's good to hear laughter in the house, instead of all the banging workmen! But have we no cakes to go with the sweet tea for your guests, Miriam?"

"They are not guests, Miss." she said quietly. "They my family."

"Family?"

"Yes, Miss. This—"

The man lifted his head and Ursula felt her heart stop.

"Sling," she whispered.

"Yes, Miss Ursula," the deep voice, clear of all the pitch variations of adolescence. "Though I am called Henson now. And these are my children, Ada and Kali."

"Sling," she said again, reaching out her hand. "You are alive."

"Oh yes, Miss."

Ursula's hand continued to shake, even in his firm, comforting grip. He sat her in the best of the yoke backed kitchen chairs. She looked from him to Miriam, and back again, still not believing. Miriam eased the girls toward the corner cupboard with its sponge cakes inside.

The entrance into that other time opened. The deep, chocking urge to go silent rather than kill again returned, strong. Miriam saw it. She nodded, from her place entertaining his daughters. Tell. It was safe, now. Tell.

Ursula's voice was just above a whisper as she stared at her hands. "He described every detail of your capture. And your death. It was… unspeakable, Sling."

"And a lie. It was a lie, Miss Ursula."

"He said I was responsible. He said I killed you."

She lifted her head. His eyes were as steady and resolute as his mother's, Ursula thought.

"That was an evil thing to plant in you," his deep man's voice proclaimed, before he smiled, showing the familiar small gap between his front teeth. "Your fishing partner, that rascal child, he kept running, he got help for himself. He came north. You hear what I say, Miss Ursula?"

Miriam returned to her side, put a cup of steaming tea into her hands. "I did not know Master put that burden on you, or I would have told you when you lately come back to us. Drink up, Miss."

Ursula swallowed.

"That's the way," Miriam encouraged her. "In the root cellar. Remember, when we talked there, of that night? After you married your Lieutenant? Say you remember, Miss," she demanded now, holding her gaze.

Swallow. Swallow the tea. Find your voice again, Ursula told herself, you are frightening them. You are frightening Sling's beautiful children. But she kept feeling the leather strap, choking her life away. "Yes," she managed to whisper. "I remember thinking it strange. You sounded angry at Sling for not having sense. As if he was still alive."

"On account of he is alive, yes! My Sling is here, in New York City. A fine man named Mr. Henson, on account of he used to bring his woman, his free, learned woman a boiled egg present every morning when he was courting her. So that woman, she said, so many eggs? He must be the hen's son. Now, she said that just when he was looking for a proper name for himself! Imagine that! Good a name as any, says our Sling! So now he's Mr. Henson, with a family of his own. A free family."

"How?"

"This city is a big place, Miss," Sling assured her. "Big enough to hold a whole colony of us, north of here. And I could write, thanks to your mama allowing me to sit alongside you at her lessons. And you never lording your learning over me, but passing it on, all patient like to this wild one. Wrote my own free papers, first thing, here in this city. Wrote them for others, to make my way. Found my Lena, my wife, my girls' mama, working at the print shop when I needed more ink. Made friends with a chicken, so's I could get a little courting conversation every morning. Sent word south to my mother, over the years.

"We are all in hiding now, Mama says, even you. We are all hoping for the war to be done and the coming Jubilo."

Miriam's eyes shone, but that familiar set of her jaw grew firm. "I hold my secrets, to keep my boy and his family safe," she said. "You understand secrets, Miss."

"I do," Ursula breathed out.

Sling nodded, laughing. "I am before you now, and most grateful for your fetching my mama north to us." His expression changed. "Oh no, please, Miss Ursula, don't take on."

His smaller daughter approached, giving up her new plaything to him. He shook the magic out of his mother's mouse, and handed the handkerchief to her.

Ursula blew her nose heartily and saw blurred images of both little girls staring at them from Miriam's skirts.

"Bibi, why is the white lady and Daddy both crying now?" Ada asked her grandmother.

Chapter 39

"They must stay here. Our third and fourth floors, if we can make them an appealing home."

"You think so, Miss?"

Ursula stifled a girlish giggle at the look on Miriam's face. "Well, of course they must! Sling and his family have been living in abodes of their own making up in that wild land. Who else will make sure the new roof remains snug over us?"

"Miss Ursula, you don't owe my family."

"But I do. For years gone by. Years they should have known you. For your daughters, Miriam, and what they endured. We must find them too. But for now, thanks to Sling— oh I beg your pardon, that is, Mr. Henson— and his Lena, you will have some of your family back with you. And Lena's parents, they are so wonderful with the children, they must join us too! Miriam, be sensible, we need help to run this household. We'll make Mr. Henson head of the Carriage House staff, and Lena the cook staff. You will be head of household, of course. They will know of more people to hire, will they not?"

Miriam sighed. "I expect so, Miss Ursula, as the city politicians are fixing to tear down their home and all those around to make way for that fancy park uptown."

"How is that possible? Do they hold title?"

"They do, Miss, as do most of their neighbors."

"How unjust! How many families? I shall have a word with Mr. Gardner."

Miriam gave her the sternest look Ursula remembered from her childhood. "Fighting those high and mighty city folk would not be good for keeping yourself private and mysterious, Miss, like your Mr. Gardner has instructed of us.”

“Of course. How foolish of me. We will have to put the credit and blame on Mr. Gardner himself in those endeavors, shall we? He is a good man, and will not mind, I think. For now we can at least find places for a staff to help us all get properly settled. Now come, Mr. Gardner will be here soon for our excursion along the Fourteenth Street shops. Help me choose comfortable bedding for all.”

Miriam shook her head, even as she reached for their capes. “You may be as rich as God, Miss Ursula. But, please have more care, you still be a woman.”

“With wonderful champions.”

“That I grant you. So we must keep them safe, too.”

Ursula stared out kitchen’s window, into the garden. The war battles would be starting up again soon in earnest. After the December battle at Fredericksburg, she had read of skirmishes, none involving the Army of the Potomac. “Of course, you are right. Men do such terrible things to each other.”

“I am still getting used to all this, Miss, being so far away from our troubles, and the war.”

“Yes. I am too, my dear friend.”

“But you got a summer time baby coming. Summer babies always lucky.”

Ursula laughed. “Are they? Well, we must look more welcoming to our new little member of the household! New hats first, for us both, long overdue. So we can refashion ourselves as proper, and mostly quiet-living Gramercy Park matrons.”

Miriam squeezed her offered hand. “Mostly,” she echoed.

Chapter 40

Spring 1863

March, 1863

"I have not seen the crepe myrtle flower this far north. But it has fallen under your spell, Mrs. Major."

Ursula looked up, no longer on guard when she heard the beautiful modulation of his voice that so reminded her of Rowan's. But it was without Rowen's lightness. This man, her neighbor who lived at number twenty-eight, was, after all, a tragedian. The dappled sunlight through the flowering tree's branches only increased the beauty of his features by casting half of them in mysterious shadow. She looked past his perfectly tailored clothing, made mournful by his widower's black armband, and up through the tree's branches to the sun.

"It is Miriam who has been digging and feeding this beauty since the last snow, Mr. Booth. She only allows me care of my medicinals."

"You are a formidable duo, then. I must present your aide-de-camp with my compliments. And to you, a thanks for sending over your tea packet."

"Your cough is better?"

"My cough is gone. And my throat is clear."

"Camomile is soothing."

"But combining it with slippery elm and orange peel made it a source of pleasure to drink, and have me more appealing to my family and fellows. Those poor souls made themselves bear garlic, garlic, and more garlic over my illnesses!"

"Fellows? Fellow actors? You are planning a performance then?"

His wide brow furrowed. "No. I am not yet ready. But my family is hatching a scheme. One I hope appeals to you, as we would invite you to participate in our conspiracy."

The smile left her face. The Booths were from her native Maryland, something both Edwin and his sister Asia had already picked up from her own manner of speech. Ursula did not know their political allegiances, here in New York, which some called a city of sedition. What was this talk of conspiracies? Did he know anything of her time in Maryland and Washington? Did he somehow learn of the suspicions against her? She felt herself swaying.

"My dear lady! What have I done?" He suddenly had her elbows and was drawing her up from her place among her plantings. And noticing something, she saw it in those wide, expressive eyes that she was sure transmitted towering emotions to the back galleries of theaters. "Why, Mrs. Major," he said in a hushed whisper, "you are expecting a child?"

"Yes," she said, thinking what a wonder Lena's mother was with a needle, to keep her widening waist an almost secret for so many months.

He brought her to a wrought iron bench and sat close beside her. "What a comfort that must be."

Ursula looked at her hands. She did not like her black mourning clothes. She did not like even pretending Rowan was dead. Especially to this man, who had so recently buried his own wife. But his words were true. Say it. Go beyond your fear, she told herself. Ursula, speak.

"Yes, it is a comfort."

"Did your husband know of the child?"

"No. No he did not." Does not. Oh, Rowan.

The actor patted her hand. Ursula looked into his eyes, and felt badly only for him, victim of her deception. She smiled. "I am so sorry I frightened you. I am well, if a bit unsteady at times, getting used to my new girth."

"Oh, be not at all concerned about me, dear lady. Ah, but this is wonderful for us, for all your neighbors here in our little Gramercy community. A playmate for my little Edwina. I must tell my sister! With your permission, of course. Shall I walk you to your door first? Or ask Miriam or Lena to come and see to you?"

"No, no, I am quite well."

"Why, of course you are! My Mollie, she bloomed with health as we waited for Edwina. Trudging through my European tour with me, a different city every night! And then our triumphant journey across the Atlantic and home, neither she nor the baby even seasick. That was why I did not think to come up to Boston, when Mollie wrote that she was ill. She asked me to come, but I thought not to rush, she was such a hardy lass, my Mollie."

The energy was gone from a handsome face, now devoured by melancholy.

Ursula patted their hands. "I am so sorry."

His wide, powerful brow furrowed again and he shook his head. "It ends like this, the telling of it, always, mired in that day, learning it was too late, that I did not even hear her farewell. And you sit in this beautiful place, comforting me, when your own was taken from us, also in the prime of his life. And not by sickness, but in this deliberate slaughter our countrymen have wrought against each other."

"Stop, please." Do not make it real. Do not take her sergeant, her beautiful angel of death, with his tin whistle. Do not bring him down with the others they looked after together.

"Forgive me. Oh my dear. Forgive me."

High above, in the branches of the flowering tree, a robin sang out.

"Of course. We must both battle our blue devils, Mr. Booth, for the sake of the children left in our care."

"Yes, you are right."

The fear returned, that she was being brought into a circle of deception, of danger to herself, her family. "Mr. Booth. Please tell me of your request."

"Request?"

"Your 'conspiracy?'"

"Oh, do not think on it. I could not possibly ask it of you, knowing your delicate state."

"I am not ill, sir, as you yourself have assured me."

"Now you sound like my Mollie, always knowing the show must go on. She was a fine actress, I am sure you would have been fast friends. And, yes, of course she would wish me to enlist your talented fingers in our scheme. I do not know if I will ever appear on stage again. But we are planning to raise money, with a single benefit performance, my family and I, so that a statue of Shakespeare may be placed in the new Central Park. Would that not be grand?"

Ursula smiled brightly, fighting off her distrust of people who would displace the poor to have their riding and strolling ground. And would the park truly be open to all? "A place we can celebrate the beauty, the humanity Mr. Shakespeare saw in all of us," she managed. "I think a tribute is a wonderful idea, Mr. Booth."

"You do understand! Our own Poet's Corner, like the one they have in Westminster Cathedral in England. But outside, where the air, and nature itself, belongs to us all. And therefore, American in character."

Ursula laughed out loud. "A grand scheme indeed. How might I help?"

"Well, my brothers Junius, Johnny and I are concocting the performance. We have never been on stage all three of us together, between touring and Johnny's new passion for Pennsylvania oil fields. We thought that all of us together might help fill the theater. We have a more selfish motive, I will admit, as the performance is also a way for my brother-in-law and I to let patrons know that the Winter Garden is heading away from the musicals and lighter fare towards more classical presentations under our management. But we would send all the proceeds towards the statue.

"Now of course, we cannot decide on which of the plays might suit our combined abilities best. So my sister Asia suggested we invite you to our meeting and rehearsals.

She thinks your lovely melodies on the piano will calm our heated political differences as well as our expressions of preference among the plays."

Ursula tried to hide her smile. The Booths were notorious for their artistic temperaments. Asia was a wise woman.

"I shall be most happy to assist in your endeavor," Ursula assured her neighbor.

* * *

Ursula's fingers left the keyboard. She was happy she'd insisted on bringing the piano tuner in earlier in the week, for the tone of the Booths' instrument was now rich and true.

"Mrs. Major, you are far beyond the best we've ever experienced in our parlor practices. You impart the Bard himself through your glorious interpretations of Schumann. I declare you are their own, their very own Erato with your glorious accompaniment!"

"I hardly think so, Mr. Booth."

"What say you, family? Shall we take Mrs. Major on stage with us, with a lyre and a crown of roses?"

"Leave our poor neighbor a shred of dignity, Johnny," his sister admonished.

Ursula enjoyed the company of the whole handsome and gifted family. But where brother Johnny Wilkes was, on her first impression, charming, and Junius beamed with his intelligence, her neighbor Edwin lead with his kindness. He remained her favorite. She turned to him now.

"Have you decided on Hamlet, then, with its wonderful lyric passages?" she asked him.

It was Junius who answered. "We feel it may be too foreign and mystical between Danish court setting and ghosts," he replied.

Asia offered Ursula a tray of lemon tarts. "And it highlights Edwin's gifts rather too largely for the other scene-stealers!" she confided with a wink, drawing both exaggerated sneers and guffaws from her siblings.

189

"We have Julius Caesar on the reading list next," Edwin explained. "It has a more familiar senate and republic in danger from the forces of tyranny. Perhaps it might be more appropriate for our American-themed Shakespeare in the park."

"…And with enough grand speeches for them all!" Asia was still at Ursula's ear, prompting a giggle.

Chapter 41

Frederick, Maryland
March 1863

The sound was deafening. Rowan struggled with his gut clenching reaction to the sight of the stone bridge. Not that bridge, he reminded himself again, not the one whose blasted fragments were still embedded in his flesh. This bridge was crowded with townspeople and farmers whose loyalties he could predict based on their reaction to the sight of Union uniforms. Not his own exotic one, which had regiments on both sides, but the blue-coated men. So much the better. He could watch civilians. Watch them all. For weapons, for bursts of anger. He wanted desperately to be back among his men, who were boisterous and unruly but who would defend him in any fight.

There it was again, assaulting his ears. "Preserves! Pickled beets here! Fresh wrapped butter! Home goods! Oddities! Come over! Visit my tent!" Rowan felt the sweat lining his brow, although all around him were still bundled against the damp cold. He quickly added some dandelion greens to his sack of cabbages, paid the farmer and caught up to Jonathan.

"What are we doing here?" he demanded.

"We are on furlough, brother. Shopping for vegetables. For the health of our company. Relax."

"With all this yelling?"

"It is not yelling, it's selling. Do you not have market days in Canada?"

"Not as loud."

"Silas and Aaron will appreciate those cabbages and greens for their soups. Did you fill the sack? Did you not pay the first price offered? Look, there's the first of the asparagus. Buy a few pounds. I am heading for the herbals, one of them will surely be there."

"One of—?"

"The ones who can help us get Ursula back! Her convent is a scarce three miles away. What kind of spy are you?"

"No kind. We are regular army now, Jonathan. I am finished with—"

Jonathan spun on his heel to face him. "When we are camped so close to her home of the last fourteen years? Are you finished with her, then? Finished with my sister?"

"Of course not, but—"

"Listen. The government men, because of the manner of her departure, they have decided on her guilt. Why have we heard nothing of their progress?"

"Because the government men have concluded that we helped spirit Ursula and Miriam away."

"Which I did not. Did you?"

"How many times are you going to ask me that? No!"

"I need to make sure you remain heartbroken. But not… well, worried."

"Worried?"

"That she did not reach where you sent her."

"Jonathan, I am your sister's husband. I love her. And respect the brave woman who accompanies her. Why am I not permitted to be worried about them?"

"Because it is a waste of our meager resources. Especially yours. I do not like the look of you today. What's wrong with you? One of your headaches?"

"No." Rowan did not know how to find words for the malady that a yell, the sight of a bridge, a smell could set off, causing his heart to race, his mind to plunge into a fog of melancholy.

"We must get some of those greens into you. Listen, kin. My sister is not used to the wider world, but she is in Miriam's blessed company. A more formidable woman I had not encountered until the Widow Picard descended on us. Miriam and my sister will take care of each other, wherever they have landed. Now, if those government jackals have gone on to new adventures in espionage, we will get no help from them. We are on our own in the task of clearing Ursula, exonerating the family name. Your excellent sister Madame Picard understands, she is doing her part."

Rowan grunted. "I will not forgive her for taking your place at Fenwick Pines, so you can plague me for the rest of the war."

"If Lincoln had any sense, it is she who should have replaced McClellan. But she appears content to supervise the care of the poor devils drilling and those recovering from their Fredericksburg wounds in our small corner of the world."

"When she is not sailing in Ratchitt's Bay with Captain Kane."

"He's in your letters from her too? Now that is interesting."

"How much do you know of this man?"

"That he loved our mother and Ursula's father. That love does not extend to any Kingsley, except me. There was always mystery about the man who sailed in and out of our childhood. But I am firm in the belief that he would put his hand in the fire for us." Jonathan grinned suddenly. "Now, with his squeezebox at the ready, you can form a trio with Marie Madeline when the war is over, and thus keep a better eye on him, if he vies to change Madame Picard's name yet again."

"That's absurd! Marie Madeline is finished with husbands!"

"She and her sisters had their hands full with you to raise up. But you're done at last, and in my sister's charge."

"Your sister in hiding."

"Only until we can find how she's been slandered. Ursula has not betrayed us or our country, brother! You need to get over your bruised feelings and help me to free her of suspicion so we can find her!"

Rowan felt a knot loosening in his chest. "Yes. Yes, of course, you are right."

"I may not be as handy with a Bowie knife as the mad new recruits of our company, but I do have some redeeming qualities. Now. The road to Ursula lies in finding those who planted troop plans in her quarters at the nunnery and in Washington. The late unlamented Colonel Blanchard was working with someone. And trying to connect Ursula. I'm thinking they wanted to enlist my sister in their efforts."

"Jonathan, the man was going to kill her."

"Exactly. Why? Perhaps she had refused, perhaps she was discovering something. If only we had talked with her more. I was so afraid for her health, afraid that my father would lock her away from me again."

"We did our best. She did her best at the remembering."

"That farmer is smiling too wide. How much did you give them for those cabbages? Wait, never mind. At last. There she is!"

"There who is?"

But Jonathan was already bounding over to a small round woman in a brown veil. She stood behind a stall offering glass bottles of peach brandy, tinctures and small pots of herbs for sale. Behind her another nun was busy knitting. Their veil's color signified the kind of nuns who served the others. These were the ones let out of the cloister, to provide. The ones who nursed the wounded, over that month after Antietam. Rowan closed his eyes, tried to pick up scents, voices, to remember them from his sightless days.

"Sister Michaela!" Jonathan called. "You've got the herbs going again, and looking healthy I see."

"Why, Mr. Kingsley! Have you gone and joined the circus?"

"The army, Sister, although a decidedly eccentric company within."

"The dashing Zouaves, of course. We have seen your like and know you are neither jugglers nor acrobats, rest assured, my dear." She patted his arm. "We have missed your visits to our herbalist, whose gardens have, yes, flourished even in my own rude care." She stood back. "And who is your companion in arms?"

"It's Sergeant Buckley, Sister, do you not know him? Of the infernal tin whistle and many bandages? He is my superior officer, whilst, lo and behold, I now have his stripes."

The woman's hand covered her mouth as her laughing eyes turned sober. "Sergeant Buckley. Who went through the fire for her?"

"Only the smoke, Sister," Rowan said.

"But, is it possible that this handsome ghost before me is her Sergeant Buckley?"

Jonathan frowned. "He's a lieutenant now, Sister Michaelita. Do not make him even more full of his own accomplishments. Look," he tapped at his stripes, "I'm the sergeant."

But she continued staring at Rowan, her fingers hovering around his scarred cheek. "And your sight restored? A miracle, surely."

"A miracle of good care," Rowan said gently. "Beside the Shenandoah and the Potomac rivers both."

Jonathan came between them. "Did Sister Philomena not tell you all that transpired in Washington upon her return from the capitol city?"

"Why, no, sir. As Sister Philomena has not returned to us."

"Has she not?" Rowan asked.

Darting eyes, then a slight quiver played around the sister's lips.

Jonathan lowered his voice. "Perhaps you might leave your stall in your good neighbor's care, and have a walk along the canal with us?" he asked.

The knitting sister fashioning fingerless gloves from her wool skeins nodded her assent.

Rowan did not have a sense of either woman ever gliding by him on the convent's grounds. But he now sensed in Sister Michaelita an ally. She took his arm as they walked. He let Jonathan do the talking as he scanned the canal's toe path for enemies.

"What has happened in Washington, sir? She is well, our Ursula?" she asked him quietly.

"I cannot say, Sister. She is lost to us."

Missing," Jonathan corrected.

"Missing? Oh, how dreadful. This is not what Raphaela wished for her, not at all."

"Sister Raphaela?" Jonathan asked quietly. "Who first allowed me inside your walls?"

"Oh, she did much more than that, young man! She stood up to the motherhouse and the bishop himself on your sister's behalf. We were her sanctuary, when first she came to us. But Sister Raphaela was firm in the belief that our life, either in service or cloistered, was not God's will for Ursula. That you were her angel, just as your father, well—"

"Wanted to bend her and her fortune towards his will," Jonathan finished for her.

"He did bend her. He brought her here at a most dire time in her young life." She looked up at Rowan, "My dears, listen to me, now. I came to our order after my husband and children were killed in the wreck of a train. The sisters gave me solace, and community, and I chose to make my life with them. But Ursula gave up her will inside our walls. It is why it can take the desperate, too-young ones so many years to fully profess, you see? Gratitude is not choice. Raphaela knew it. That is why she fought for your visits, Mr. Kingsley, as vehemently as she fought against your father...well, ever getting near her."

Jonathan nodded. "And when Sister Raphaela died, my sister lost her champion."

"But Ursula was coming into her own by then. Nudged along by you, of course."

"The bishop was at our motherhouse, raving about 'the colossal nerve of her seduction,' I'm sorry to inform you, Sergeant Buckley. He was much more disquieted by affectionate regard than he was by our convent being involved in a breach of war neutrality. It was affection, was it not, sir? I noticed the change in her over your time with us. So much she had managed to quiet, to blunt, was coming alive again." She stopped walking and faced Rowan. "You care for our Ursula?"

"More than my life, Sister. And she has married me."

"Oh? Oh, how grand. They did not tell us that part of their terrible scandal! My dears, not all of us feel the bishop's notion of a deep shame brought down upon us all when Ursula was lost to us."

Jonathan snorted. "When her fortune was lost, more likely."

"There may be truth in what you say, sir." She cocked her head sideways. "You are a very different man from your father, you do know that, Mr. Kingsley?"

"And you are hardly only the obedient servant of your order, content to perform your duties without eyes, ears, or thoughts that are your own, Sister Michaelita."

"Hmm, should I thank you, sir?"

"As it is a wholehearted compliment, yes. And I pray to remain very unlike my father."

The nun's bright eyes grew suddenly troubled. "There is no possibility, that is to say, our Ursula could not possibly be with him at present, sir?"

"No, Sister. As she left of her own will."

The eyes calmed. "Good. She will find you again, Mr. Kingsley. Just as you found her."

"It is the dearest wish of two men who are useless louts without her, Sister. But we need to do more now. We need to have her returned to us cleared of blame for this breech of neutrality. She is suspected of treason against the federal government."

The small nun's eyes lit with more understanding. "So that is also why the bishop has made so many visits of late? And why Philomena did not return from Washington? We thought it was to comfort her family, after the loss of her nephew."

"Her nephew?"

"Yes. Her sister's son. Colonel Blanchard."

The hard slap across his face stung Rowan again. He'd thought it stemmed from the shock of the sudden violence in a place of healing. "Murderer" she had screamed. He'd killed a man in the woman's family.

Jonathan stopped. "Those two. They were in league. I should have seen it. I should have known. Colonel Blanchard pulled Ursula towards his needs, once Philomena was banished to kitchen duty in Washington. He asked for her, trusted her scissors only to cut away his bandaging."

"They told us he died of his wounds, there in Washington, Mr. Kingsley."

Jonathan shot a quick glance at Rowan. "He is dead. But shot for a spy," he pronounced quietly.

"Spy? We were harboring a spy?"

"I speak of the hospital in Washington, Sister."

"But we cared for him at the convent, after Antietam. Philomena wrote letters for him, to her sister, because of his hand's damage."

"Where were these letters bound, Sister?"

"Why, Richmond."

"Her sister lives in Richmond?"

"Yes. A family priest stayed with us in the convent after the battle. He promised to deliver his letters. Called himself her "express rider service.""

"And this priest? What was his name?"

"Durnell. Yes, Father Durnell. Loved my stewed berries. But he always came and went so quickly."

"Those letters contained information. About troop movements."

"We need to find this priest, Sister. And Sister Philomena."

"Oh I'm afraid that's hardly possible. Philomena insisted on carrying word of her loved one's demise back to his mother. And no one's heard a word from either her or Father Durnell since."

* * *

Sister Michaela returned to her stall. Jonathan paced. Rowan hated it when Jonathan paced.

"We must find Philomena and the priest, bring them to Washington."

"How?"

"Yes, yes! How?" More pacing. Rowan closed the lids down on his eyes, but heard Jonathan stop abruptly. "Offer ourselves as spies!"

"In Richmond? We infiltrate the heart of the Confederacy?"

"Yes! We make Aaron and Silas part of it! They are wonderful disseminators. They will play the part of our manservants."

"Jonathan. Aaron and Silas do not work for us. They are in service to the army, the same as we are."

His brother-in-law sighed elaborately. "A dead end, then?"

"Yes, for now, we are under the army's command."

"Shall I desert?"

"Good God. You will do no such thing."

"But after I explain—"

"They will give you no time to explain. And even should you find that nun and priest, if he is a priest, those two would be delighted to turn you over to the other side. You will be shot. They may wait until dawn, in consideration you are from a border state, of course."

Jonathan's frown of concentration deepened. "And when Ursula learns of that, she will hunt you down, shoot you, before she dies of grief over the both of us." Suddenly, he stopped pacing and smiled brightly. "There. We have our solution, kin. A reunion for all in heaven."

Rowan growled. "Good plan."

"No." Jonathan reconsidered his own strategy. "There are no babies in that plan."

"Babies?"

"Yes. You two do know how to make babies, do you not? But you shall not be left to your own devices to raise them properly."

Chapter 42

Spacious Firmament Orphan's Asylum
April, 1863

In this city of immigrants, too many of them reminded Ursula of Rowan.

As soon as they alighted from the carriage, a barrel chested policeman in his brasses and blue visored cap held up an umbrella high to shelter both her and Miriam, leaving only himself pelted with rain. The resemblance was not his looks, which favored the shorter in stature, red-headed Irish and not Rowan's tall, black haired variety. It was the police sergeant's eyes that were like her husband's— seared by suffering, but warmed with amusement.

"Ah, and didn't the matrons Bigelow say to expect you ladies this morning? Let me get you inside, then!" he proclaimed. "Or Dr. Walker will have two patients coughing!"

"Are any children ill, sir?" Miriam asked.

"No, no! Mr. Bell assures us all the new graduates are hale and hearty."

He walked behind them all the way up the steps of the Spacious Firmament Orphan's Asylum. Under its portico, he reached out and pulled the bell. "Two more graduates are heading down toward Gramercy Park this day, I hear?"

"They are indeed. To neighbors in need of help with children and pies."

"Not one in the other, I hope!"

Miriam hid her smile behind her hand as Ursula shook her head, laughing. "Quite separate, I assure you. Now, none of your dark humor in front of our graduates, they are quite worried enough as they begin to make their own way in the world."

"Sergeant Harrigan!" Hester Bigelow proclaimed at the door. "Won't you join us to attend this morning's graduation?"

"Nothing would please me more, but I must be back on the watch, dear lady," he answered, looking up at the gracious landing's tall windows to the faces peering out, hands waving. Behind them stood Mr. Bell, assistant of Dr. Walker.

"Ah, now that man is too serious," the policeman observed with what Ursula took to be a studied casualness. "Maybe another trip into the wilds of Brooklyn with your family, Mrs. Henson? Would that do the trick. think you?"

Miriam looked down at her hands. "Such nonsense!" she muttered.

But was it? Had the twinkle-eyed police officer surmised a fondness between Miriam and Mr. Bell, Ursula wondered.

"Here's a little luck for Henry and Lily as they set out in the wider world." A flash of two silver coins passed between Sergeant Harrigan and Hester Bigelow. He touched his hat and almost danced back down the steps.

The elderly matron frowned and shook her head. "Sister," she called within. "Our Sergeant is up to his tricks!" She leaned closer to Miriam, "But it is true that Mr. Bell has not stopped going on about the healthful effects of pic-nicing at your son's plot of farmland, Mrs. Henson," she confided.

Miriam shook her head, muttering "Nonsense!" again.

Yes, the shy chemist and Miriam were forming an attachment! How grand. How perfectly wonderful, Ursula thought. She should have seen it. She must encourage it. Miriam deserved a beautiful life that included the love of a good man.

Things were changing so quickly since they had come to New York. Her world was widening as fast as her body was expanding. Her moving, kicking baby now reminded her of more changes to come. Suddenly, a wave of sadness threatened to overwhelm her. What would she do without Miriam? And where was Rowan, her own sergeant?

Miriam patted her hand. The woman was all too accomplished at reading her moods. Ursula offered a quick prayer for Rowan's health and safety, knowing he, like the kind-hearted metropolitan policeman, walked with grace through any trouble. Could she do any less, here in wartime?

Chapter 43

Camp Hicks, Maryland
April 1863

Captain Merritt tapped his stopwatch and smiled. The drill was complete. The designated squad within company D gained on the time it took to load their carbine-style two-band muskets on their backs, turned prone or rise only to their knees, and fire off a single volley. Then they reached for their bowie knives and climbed the small bluff to an imagined opposing enemies to finish them off.

Rowan chose these Pennsylvania dock workers and street fighters, more used to a punch-up than a shootout, for this specialized squad duty. But would they have the sand to go hand to hand with guardians of the immense firepower of heavy artillery? He had placed a sprinkling of combat veterans among them, but he could not be sure.

His captain approached. "I believe we have a decent squad of cannon killers, lieutenant," he said.

Sergeant Kingsley lifted his brow towards the rim of his cap and chèchia headdress, tilted, un-regulation style, at an angle. What was the use? There was nothing regulation about his brother-in-law, just as there was nothing regulation about Captain Merritt's Zuzus.

Chapter 44

East Side Docks, Manhattan
April 11, 1863

The ferryman looked impatient to leave. Ursula stepped towards the remaining plants.

Miriam blocked her way. "You will lift none of those, Miss Ursula!"

"But surely, the herbals—"

"None I say! Do not make me regret I allowed you a little air on the docks instead of your bench and garden."

"I have weeded every garden in the common until all my neighbors are ready to shoo me into their dustbins, Miriam."

"Justly so! You got to fight those early nesting inclinations so the little one comes all finished and hearty and ready to greet the world. Now take the air while the children and I get the rest of the plants on board."

Ursula felt a great tumble inside her. The baby was on Miriam's side of the issue too. Ursula felt quite outnumbered as a cool breeze blew her light cape around her shoulders.

"Wise words."

She turned to see Captain Kane. He took her jawline in his hand and planted a kiss on her forehead before removing his coat and placing it across her arms.

Special duty, I trust you with my coat. Now, sit."

He joined the others loading the start of medicinal gardens at the large settlement of free people across the river in Brooklyn.

Miriam was visiting them often, now that the Hensons had bought their farm. The house was almost complete. A big house, bigger than they had planned, at Ursula's urging. For a growing family, for harvest time boarding of orphans in need of open space, and good green earth.

Miriam seldom mentioned Dr. Walker's shy assistant, Mr. Bell, the bespeckled chemist of his drug store, who now took the small box of medicinal herbs from her outstretched hands. But he and Miriam consulted with each other often on remedies. And he smiled more in her company.

"Mr. Bell," Ursula called out to him. "You will ask Mr. Willoughby at the cooperage if he has room for two new apprentices? Cato and Ned show fine skill with woodworking, do you not agree?"

"Yes, Ma'am, I will tell him so. And if he hesitates, I will tell him to expect a visit from you."

Miriam blasted out a laugh. "That should turn that sourpuss Willoughby around!" she proclaimed.

Mr. Bell's smile widened. Ursula did not mind if his merriment came at her expense.

Brooklyn was so much more quiet, leafy and peaceful than Manhattan, as charming as their small and lovely Gramercy Park was. Ursula wondered if she would lose Miriam and her whole family to both the Brooklyn farm and her admirer. Is that why the family trained the graduates of the orphan asylum in the household duties at the Gramercy Park house with such care? To take over for them?

The thought pained Ursula. It was a selfish pain, born of her own loneliness. After the baby comes, she must talk with Miriam on her own family's dreams, and the needs of her own heart.

Captain Kane returned from helping the ferry to cast off into the East river. "Mr. Gardner is worried about you."

"Why?"

"He says you have not consulted with the physician he recommended."

"These things are better left to the womenfolk, Captain. Miriam is a skilled midwife, as was her mother before her. And you see how she bullies me towards her will."

"But it is your first baby. Terra incognito."

It was not, but only Miriam knew that most guarded of her secrets. "It will hardly be Miriam's first attended birth, sir. Most importantly, I feel safe in her care."

Her friend sighed hard. "I will report back to Mr. Gardner and try to keep him at bay."

She patted his hand. "You are a good godfather."

He grinned wide. "I hope to be. And I take a measureless pride in the honor."

How she loved pleasing Captain Kane. She hoped Rowan would approve of the choice of the man who delivered her to this new life in the North, so different than the one she had agreed to with Rowan's family in Quebec. Who else would she ask to dote on her little one?

"I do not like the look of that sky. Storm's coming," Captain Kane interrupted her wandering thoughts. "And your esteemed midwife has left you in my care until she returns from her son's."

"Surely there is no need."

"Not need. Request, from the woman, I remind you, that you have put in charge of your care. I am honored by her trust."

"Well. I am captured, then."

They walked along the dock to a quiet spot under a budding willow tree. Lucius Kane knew may such spots, Ursula surmised, close to his ports, all over the world. Had her father known them too?

I have two things for you, Ursula."

"Yes?"

"The first, well. I do not mean to frighten you, but with your household not always gathered about you, and with me setting off on the water again soon…"

He placed a small revolver in her dwindling lap.

"Captain Kare, surely there is no need for this."

"Surely." He smiled. "Except that it would make me feel better if I knew you allowed me to teach you the use of this firearm. And if you promised me that you would keep it within reach, always, my health while we are apart, would benefit."

"Well. If it is a matter of your health."

"It is a powerful device. But simple to use and maintain."

Ursula slipped the firearm into her side pocket.

"Thank you for easing the worry of this rapidly aging godfather. I shall plague you with its use and upkeep later today. My second duty is much more pleasant. I have a letter for you, Ursula."

"A letter? Captain, is Rowan—?"

"Your husband is well. But I expect you will learn more in the letter. It is from Madame Picard."

"Madame Picard writes to you from Canada?"

"They kept her at Fenwick Pines as hostage once they discovered you had gone. Then, well, read the letter, which she writes to her sisters, of which you are one, are you not? She has now quite turned over the tables on her keepers. And she has surmised the seafaring method of your deliverance, hence her trust in me."

A soft drizzle began falling. Ursula barely noticed it. Captain Kane stood.

"Come with me, dear heart. You and I shall visit Downing's Oyster house for to keep you dry and fed. Then you may read." He held up his hand before Ursula could object, "Also part of your midwife's directive."

The bustling oyster establishment seemed the worst place for Ursula to read the letter. But the kind-eyed man at the entrance made a deep bow and led them to a beautifully appointed private room. Perhaps he had noticed her pregnancy, even though the current fashion's cape bodices shawls, along with Lena's deft seamstress fingers continued to work magic. But her appetite would be a good hint. Soon she was finishing a bowl of the best oyster soup she had ever tasted.

"My." Ursula looked up into delighted eyes of Lucius Kane, "I did not realize how hungry I was."

"You're under the spell of the Downing family, who have served Charles Dickens, and sent oysters to Queen Victoria."

She blinked. "Truly?"

"Mr. Thomas Downing, the founder of this establishment, has the gold chronometer watch Her Majesty bestowed on him in thanks."

A soft knock at the room's door produced two handsome black men, one of middle years with a tall and commanding presence. and the other of older years.

"Mrs. Major, may I introduce you to Thomas and George Downing?"

The younger man spoke close to his father's ear. "This is Captain Martin's daughter, Daddy."

"Truly?" he echoed her astonishment from moments before, to the delight of his son and Captain Kane. "This is little Ursula?"

"Not so little these days, sir. You knew my father?"

But the older man kept staring at her as if she would disappear.

"We held him in great esteem, great esteem, dear lady," his son said. "His influence continues in this establishment, in the Seaman's Home, in our outfitting store, providing good stewards, cooks, and sailors for ships the world around. Did you know?"

"I am continuously learning of my father's good works in this city, sir. Perhaps that is why I feel so welcome here."

"And Captain Kane tells us you have his generous heart. They sing your praises at the orphan's home and your efforts towards the education of our children."

"What I do brings me joy and pleasure, sir. It is hardly worthy of praise."

It was only after the Downings had left them that Ursula voiced her concerns. "Miriam will not be pleased, Captain. She is always advising discretion and anonymity to keep our origins and recent troubles hidden."

Captain Kane smiled. "This is a city of one million people. It is also full of our army's widows. And rest assured, the Downing family knows how to keep secrets."

He handed Ursula the letter, addressed "to my sisters" in Marie-Madeline's bold, long and graceful handwriting. At last. She opened it carefully and read.

My Dear Ones—

I write to you in English for your continued study and edification. I am employing the language daily here, as no one in this country seems to be learned enough in where their hallowed principles come from to read them in the original language of Descartes, Voltaire, and Rousseau!

Never mind, as they say here when they desire the subject to be changed. You see? I add to our arsenal of understanding the English and the Irish and now American's expressions. I report on practical matters of my extended sojourn here at Fenwick Pines in the state of Maryland. The crops, under the able stewardship of young Jonathan Kingsley, our new brother by marriage, they were changed from tobacco to sustenance years ago. The result? Last harvest stores now provide well for our growing numbers. Following the battle at Fredericksburg, we became a place of care for the wounded of that conflict. Our staff has proved well up to the task and we all go about our duties with compassion, in hopes that some caring souls are providing the same for our own loved ones in the field of encampment.

Now we have Spring planting in the ground as well. Do you think our new brother-in-law has proven himself wise in leaving the business of the estate in my hands over his term of enlistment? You know I will tolerate only one answer to this question, yes? Jonathan Kingsley now serves with our brother in his regiment of soldiers trained in the superior French of Algiers style. He writes that both are in good health as they go about their duties in the cause of the Union of the United States.

I did not anticipate that I would also serve in this cause so close to our brother's heart, but it has proved an interesting adventure in many ways.

Were I to write to our new sister, his esteemed wife, I would tell her that all is well in her childhood home, that the time for justice in her own and her country's cause is at hand, I feel closer to it every day. I would conclude that our parting is painful but not forever, here in these dangerous times.

How I long for when we are all together and it matters not where. As deep as the ties of home are, the bonds among us were forged in fire. They will remain strong forever.

Your loving sister,
Marie-Madeline Belanger Turpin Guyer Picard

Chapter 45

Summer 1863

Camp Hicks, Maryland
June 1863

The colonel swung down from the saddle and clapped their shoulders in turn. "This horse! I beg your pardon for my initial doubts regarding her size."

Jonathan's smile went lopsided "Hermia will serve you well, sir. Though she be but little, she is fierce."

"You have found me the perfect battle companion. Again, gentlemen, I am most pleased!"

Rowan stroked the neck of the mare before she was trotted off to serve the regiment's colonel. "Midsummer Night's Dream?" he asked Jonathan.

"Just so. How—?"

Rowan laughed. "Mr. Shakespeare was the only Englishman allowed in the parlor of the three Maries."

"I doubt the colonel has ever set foot in any entertainment house that did not feature dancing bears."

"Well, let's hope he can keep his seat, for that horse will lead him into hell."

"Hell, is it?" Jonathan's brow quirked up. "You hear something regarding our near future, kin?"

He was not supposed to tell Jonathan what he knew. But he trusted the man. And Rowan hated secrets. "Lee's army has crossed into Pennsylvania. We must stop them and protect the capitol city. We are headed for a place called Gettysburg."

The word seemed to set the remaining horses on edge. Jonathan put down his bucket and took Rowan's shoulder. "You are entitled to one of these remaining. I have arranged to purchase Clytie for you. You are an officer. You should be riding beside our captain."

"Jonathan. I am touched beyond measure. But I need to be with the men."

"Making us keep our heads down."

"Yes, as best I can, as we are not a standard touching elbows fighting battery." He nodded towards the flurry of movements in and around the officers' tents. "As much as I would love her company, Clytie belongs in reserve for one of those fools once his mount is shot out from under him."

Jonathan growled.

"She's a fine horse, and I thank you," Rowan tried.

Aaron Price appeared, running around the edge of the fence that held the remaining horses.

"Best let me finish up here for you, Mr. Rowan, Sergeant. You're wanted over at the general's tent, sirs."

"What's going on, Aaron?"

"Caught a peddler, sir. Found papers on him, maps of the roads around, and troop numbers, formations. They are ready to shoot him for a spy, as we're on the move soon. But he claims kinship with you, Sergeant, and is asking for your company at his hearing."

* * *

Magnus Kingsley, mud-splattered and in a worn out leather coat, looked smaller to Rowan than at their last meeting. But his imperious tone was intact.

"There, look at him, serving with distinction!" he proclaimed, pointing at Jonathan. "Is it not enough that I'm sacrificing my only son to your cause? Why are you persecuting me for attempting to hire some workmen for a few hours?"

212

A group of five tattered contrabands remained silent, staring at the ground.

"Is that not right? Speak up! Was this not a misunderstanding among us?"

The officer behind the field table whose leg began a jittery thumping finally raised his head.

"And what of the horses?"

"What I was hiring these boys of the road for, of course! To gather strays for you gentlemen… strays that became untethered. And I needed to draw up a map of your locations so as to get them returned to their rightful companies, of course."

One of the runaways swayed, dropped to his knees. Jonathan knelt, took his arms, holding up bloodied wrists. "Too quick the untethering of this one, Father. Did your knife slip as you were caught? You prefer straps to chains now?" He turned to his superiors. "This man is the cruel owner of one and manager of three plantations around Mary's Heights, gentlemen. And he has a reputation for catching both runaways and freemen. He sells them further south. I would not trust a word he utters."

Rowan brought his canteen to the downed runaway, poured water over his wrists and offered him a drink. He was not much more than a child.

"May we get this fellow to the medical tent?" Jonathan asked the members of the tribunal.

"'This fellow, this fellow?'" Magnus Kingsley parroted. "You see what this cruel war has done, gentlemen? The damned abolitionists have made my son care more for a worthless black than his own father!"

Rowan approached the table and regarded the map. It included a depiction of Ursula's convent. He thought of Magnus Kingsley, standing shoulder to shoulder with Sister Philomena. In league.

"You are somehow related to this man through your wife, are you not, Lieutenant? Does he stand any higher in your esteem than his son's?"

Rowan looked over his shoulder. No sign of Jonathan. "He does not, sir. But he may have information helpful to our cause."

The impatient officer nodded to the others and began gathering papers off the table. "All right, then. We have not the time for any more deliberation. Get this man an armed escort to the capital city. Let that lot of spy detectorists sort it out."

As Magnus Kingsley was led out of the tent, Rowan saw the briefest smile flicker across his face.

Rowan approached the last of the tribunal members, who was busy scribbling. "Sir, for the Washington men: names to connect: this man with a nun named Philomena, a priest named Durnell, a dead spy, Colonel Blanchard, of a South Carolina regiment. If you would inform them, sir?"

The officer nodded, and went back to his writing.

* * *

Rowan found Jonathan at the creek, filling his canteen.

"I am tainted, kin. That people and horse thief's blood flows through my veins."

Rowan pressed his shoulder.

Jonathan's voice quieted. "Do you think they will shoot him?"

"Not yet. They are escorting him to Washington."

Jonathan stood and shoved the canteen against his chest. "Then we'd best get marching to this Gettysburg and keep the capitol city safe for his blessed firing squad, eh, brother?"

Chapter 46

June, 1863
New York City

Ursula smiled when she spotted Captain Adam Badeau's servant arrive bearing a tray of watercress sandwiches and onion tarts. She was famished. She was always famished. Her widening girth made her sit differently on the stool, but she still had her place at the piano, and her welcome at her neighbors' gatherings.

Beside the Booth guest, the wounded Captain Badeau, Mr. Thompson worked his clay. Surrounded by the beauty the sculptor was creating, the place was alive with creative energy.

Ursula completed the nocturne.

"My hand is guided by your lovely tones," Mr. Thompson maintained. "Why don't we all join our dear muse prompter in some refreshment, eh, Ned?"

The velvet draped Edwin Booth did not move from his brooding pose on the chair. He raised his head slowly, looking dazed.

"Did the Schumann stop?" he asked. "No one plays him like you, Mrs. Major. It was lovely."

"Thank you, sir. The tarts are delicious, come try one," she urged.

He leaned over, tapping his pipe on a tray. "Quite right. Must not start surrounding your beauty in gloomy smoke. And raspberry hand pies as well? Just the thing!"

"Just the thing would be you getting some use out of those well-researched Hamlet togs and trodding the boards of the stage again, my friend," Adam Badeau insisted. "I do not want the time and efforts I put into singing your praises from New York to Boston to be in vain."

"I shall endeavor to mount a production timed for when you are free of your bandages and can walk into the Winter Garden Theater, how would that be, Ad?"

"That would be splendid, Ned!"

The actor strolled around the clay model of himself as the Melancholy Dane. "Good work, Mr. Thompson," he proclaimed, "worthy of Mike Angelo!"

The sculptor finished wiping his hands and patted Ursula's arm. "Another act of the Ad and Ned entertainment, yes, Mrs. Major?"

The antics of the two reminded Ursula of the sparring between her brother and Rowan. They were now in the Union army together, despite her betrayal of their trust and affection. Would their friendship stand the test of war? She hoped they were taking care of each other.

"May I ask what rank your husband achieved, Mrs. Major?" the young invalid friend of Edwin Booth asked gently.

"He was a sergeant, sir," Ursula said carefully, finishing in her mind, he was a sergeant, he is now a lieutenant. She did not know why she played these games, but they distracted her from her nervousness with any who requested details of her widow's attire.

"And went down at…?"

"Antietam."

"Antietam? But, that was almost a year ago." He was staring at her high skirts.

Miriam sprang up from her sewing place in the room's corner. "Our Sergeant, he lasted a good little while at home down Maryland way, didn't he missus?" she interjected, startling them all. "Why he looked almost as good as you do, Captain! Was healing of his wounds fine until he, well, was, was…" She hauled out her mouse-making handkerchief and daubed her eyes.

"Gone from us, yes," Ursula finished, patting her friend's arm.

Silence overtook all the room's inhabitants before a flush-faced Captain Badeau spoke. "Your devotion does you proud. Miriam, is it not? M—my injury came further south, at the siege of New Orleans."

"You must achieve your own road to health, and honor all the fallen, sir," she said. "I hope my mistress's tea provides a comfort."

"Indeed, indeed! And I have had both care and comfort from my own man here, quite indispensable. And Mrs. Major's teas ease me into restful periods. I think I shall take my pot in my room, as I see the whirling dervish that is the younger Booth is about to make an appearance."

Captain Badeau signaled his manservant to lead his mechanical chair from the room.

Ursula tried to ignore the roll of Miriam's eyes before she returned to the corner.

True to form, John Wilkes came bounding in, waving a copy of the Herald at his sister, newly arrived with another tray of sweets.

"Look, look! There are reports of riots in the city of Detroit, Asia. It begins."

"What begins?"

"Resistance, dear sister. To this notion of conscription."

"It is not a notion. It is a policy."

"An unenforceable policy. The riots will spread, I am sure of it. New York is ripe, with all the immigrants walking off the boat and shoved into a uniform. The time will come when the North will groan at not being able to swear that they fought the South man for man! If the federals conquer, it will be by numbers only! Not by native grit, not pluck, and certainly not by devotion."

Ursula felt her spine straighten. For herself and her men, for the Booths' own houseguest, Captain Badeau, suffering the effects of his wound in the rooms beyond. "I can assure you of my husband's devotion, sir."

"I did not mean—"

"Devotion, even though he is an immigrant, born in Ireland and raised in Canada."

Chapter 47

July 1, 1863
Gettysburg

Rowan watched his men take their rest in the leafy shade. He remembered his first taste of peaches, in Jonathan's brandy, his first taste of Ursula, under the fruit's trees of her convent. Here, the peaches were still green on the trees. He wondered if their fruit would have time to ripen, or be obliterated in the coming battle.

The other Union Zouave regiments had discarded most of their uniforms for the standard Union blues, but despite all manner of headgear, Rowan was glad Merritt's Zuzus were still clad its loose-fitting, cooler cotton.

The soldiers around him wrote letters home, describing the orchard, and the cemetery that they had altered, taking up monuments and headstones from their pedestals. It was done to preserve them and honor the dead beneath them, but also because, should a shot of cannon fire strike, the pieces would likely do injury.

The stone bridge had cost Rowan an eye at Antietam. But it had brought him Ursula, who he dared not write to now, even if he knew where she was. Let her be safe. He would endure this longing for her. Only let her be safe. Others wrote their family farewells in the wake of the battle ahead. He had another gift for his Ursula. To not invite himself into those rabbit warrens of future sorrow. He had no control of what sight, smell, memory would ensnare him. But he was not going to hunt one out with a farewell letter. His job was to keep as many of his men alive as he could.

Chapter 48

July 3, 1863
Gettysburg

They were close enough to the artillery men to see the blood trickling from their ears. It was a relief when Captain Merritt called Company D further back.

"We are outgunned." he began.

"It appears so, sir."

"How is your sense of direction in this smoke, Lieutenant?"

"I keep my compass at the ready, sir."

"Good man. Our general wants an idea of how much ammunition they have left. Do you think you and a squad of your stealthy cannon killers can go around, bring back an estimation?"

"We will have a go, sir," Rowan answered. "If you would kindly ask the general to decrease the racket a tad."

His captain smiled. "I will put in that request directly. Go with God."

Rowan looked up at the blackening sky. "I don't think God is anywhere about, sir," he said. The truth was, he would take on any assignment to get away from the noise.

* * *

Their task completed, Rowan gathered the men around him in silence, behind a small natural ridge behind the enemy's lines. The smoke made his eye tear, clouding his vision. He wiped it away, reached for his compass, then turned to Jonathan, who had his sister's gift for calculation. "Are we all here, Sergeant?" he whispered.

"Yes, sir."

"Final count of cannons?"

"One hundred and seventy, sir."

Rowan looked into the faces of the rest of his squad. "Remember that number, all of you, in case some of us don't make it back behind our lines."

"Yes, sir."

"One seventy."

"I think we could steal a few of the Parrotts, here on the end," Jonathan opined mildly. "Looks like they stole them from us first."

"Not our mission, sergeant."

"Not the siege artillery, but a couple of the support pieces, surely."

"No," Rowan said more sternly. "Now, stay low and head for that copse of trees, on my command."

"But their fire numbers are considerably more than ours," McBride, one of the Pennsylvanians offered.

Not to be outdone, New Yorker Norcott chimed in. "We could dispatch the cannoers with our bowie knives. With the curve of the hill, and this racket, I don't think the rest would be wise to it until—"

"Hush!" Rowan demanded.

Three men in grey coats and butternut trousers appeared out of the smoke. Southern officers.

"What are you crazy Zuzus doing up here? You Hay's Louisiana Brigade?"

Rowan stood slowly, straightened his stance. "Ah oui, just so!" he proclaimed, leaning on his Quebecois accent and hoping it was close enough to the southern city's French. "Our commander, he requests for our small numbers to slip behind the enemy and count up their cannons of firepower, did you know?"

Jonathan stood beside him, and spoke in an exaggerated version of his Marylander drawl, "We are discussin' stealing a few cannons, while we are in the neighborhood, sirs." He thumped his chest.

The men behind him followed his gesture, but kept mercifully quiet.

The rebel officer in the middle began a slow smile. "Tell Hay it was a good notion, but late towards our purpose. Those Yankees are quieting down, hear? They are out of shot. Now get back to your brigade and prepare our advance."

"Oui! Merci beaucoup, sirs!"

A mist of smoke came between them and as it lifted the officers were gone. Rowan turned to his brother-in-law.

"Well, Sergeant, let us follow superiors' orders." He consulted his compass and led on. His still silent men closed in, moving behind Rowan like a brood of ducklings, until safely behind their lines again.

They were still huddled around Jonathan when Rowan returned from reporting the results of their mission to Captain Merritt. Jonathan approached him. "They call us Zuzus on the other side too," he said meekly.

"No more arguments," Rowan growled.

"Yes, sir. But, good God. Our disguise worked."

"We are in uniform, not disguise."

"But, still, we impersonated—"

"No. We allowed them to see whom they thought they saw."

"Yes, quite right." Jonathan laughed aloud. "You are still a terrible spy. Feel better?"

"Yes."

"Rowan. They think our artillery supplies depleted, because our side decreased the racket. For us, our mission. It was only a pause, for us to get through. They are now sending men in to our loaded cannons."

"Yes. I told Captain Merritt that. He will tell the commanders."

"We have a chance to prevail now, despite our fewer numbers."

"Aye."

"You mean oui! and eh bien, kin?"

"Hummph, one of their Pennsylvanians groused, "Rather we'd stole a cannon than be bathed in glory."

"Do not fret on that account," Jonathan assured him. "The generals will take all the credit."

"Rejoin company. Fix bayonets, prepare to charge," Rowan ordered.

Chapter 49

July 13, 1863
New York City

Standing in the high landing's front windows of the orphans' home on that airless, muggy day, Ursula thought them part of a street festival. This far uptown the surrounding neighborhoods were a mix of immigrants from Ireland, Germany, Italy. Was it a saint's day, or commemoration of a great event in their home country's history? Perhaps the Irish Catholics were celebrating moving ahead on the building of their grand cathedral on Fiftieth Street, barely more than a foundation at present.

"Look, a parade, Miss Ursula!" little Carrie cried out, and the call was soon echoed by the others who gathered around her.

It seemed exactly that. The men, women and children marched in gay steps, their clothes so colorful Ursula thought them beribboned. It must have been a trick of the afternoon light, of the window glass imperfections. Ursula heard a jaunty penny whistle, like her Rowan's helping them keep step. Yes, think of that joyous Rowan, she told herself, not the one in a ditch at Gettysburg, lying dead beside her brother, or in a makeshift hospital, crying for water, ignored. Those images she saw every evening as she poured over the continuing newspaper accounts of the battle, searching for theirs in the names of the casualties.

Below Ursula, a banner hung lifeless in the heat, no breeze to unfurl the two words that she could not yet make out. They might solve the mystery of the street parade. She called over some of the children on the upper stairs, heading to their sewing classes on the third floor's workroom, flooded with light. She urged them down to the landing to watch the parade before she helped the skilled teach the younger ones fine stitching. The older girls would use her latest investment in the school— Mr. Singer's wonderful machine.

They all gathered on the landing, watching. Until someone in the crowd below noticed them, in their trim white aprons, their fresh-washed faces.

The marchers' steps went awry, stumbled. Their ribbons were rags, Ursula realized. The band's instruments were tin pans, brickbats, coal scuttles. Then she saw the stones, pokers, shovels, tongs.

Weapons.

The morning breeze finally unfurled the banner. She read it: No Draft. A brick crashed through the window, skimming past Ursula's skirts.

"Lincolns! Little charcoaled Lincolns!"

"Look up there! A whole nest of them!"

"With their abolitionist nursemaid! Burn them down! Burn them down!"

Ursula dropped to her knees, pulling Carrie down beside her. "Come away, children," she called. "Away from the windows."

A cobblestone this time, a splash of blood across her sleeve, a scream. The sewing room doorway filled with little seamstresses.

"Under the windows and to the stairs, my darlings, follow me," Ursula called up to them.

The matrons were gathering children too, all around her, in groups, leading them toward the high basement as the pounding started.

"Bar the door!" Mrs. Bigelow commanded.

Ursula kept descending, kept counting, gathering from other spaces, the kitchen, the laundry room, the infirmary, where the aproned nurse Miss Decker stopped her.

"Best let me dress that, Miss Ursula."

"Dress?

"Your wound, Ma'am."

She looked at her sleeve 's blood, then touched her cheek. Yes, wet with blood. Her wound, not a child's. Good. "It is nothing." Two more past the infirmary doorway…one hundred and ninety seven, one hundred and ninety-eight.

"Yes, head wounds bleed more," Miss Decker said calmly. "Still, you do not want to frighten the children, do you?

"No, of course. She took the vinegar cloth from the nurse's hand and pressed it to her cheek, gasping. "And now, honey."

"Honey, Ma'am?"

"To seal it. No bandaging. Honey will do." She took the hands of two freshly dressed and aproned convalescents. Their eyes were confused, but not frightened. Brave girls. "My little friends and I will walk to the dining hall, shall we? Where we will find the honey pot and finish with me?"

Miss Decker sighed. "Yes, Ma'am."

"Two-hundred and thirty-seven. They had to add up to that number. More, the youngest, some in arms, coming down from the quiet Infant Schoolroom. Count. Keep counting. Upstairs they heard the mob enter, heard their shouts of frustration, smelled the splashing liquid on the new carpets of the schoolrooms, the whoosh of the flames, the smell of smoke. This was not about the military draft.

Ursula thought of Rowan pulling her off the bed of the burning room, getting her to the floor, where she could breathe. Yes, she remembered it now. His dear face. The calmness of his voice. She smeared the honey across her cheek. "We are below the fire. And we have a way to the street…the tradesman's doors on the north end. We are safest here, for now," Ursula told those made mute by fright. She understood that too.

There, it was achieved, the numbers: two hundred thirty-seven, with twenty-three staff. And, silence, among the children. A holy silence. How could she lose her nerve among all this bravery?

The head matron, Mrs. Bigelow, rose up from their center in the still cool dining hall. She spoke quietly.

"Children, do you believe that Almighty God can deliver you?"

Nods and whispers answered. "We do." and "He will."

"Then I wish you to pray to God to protect you from this mob. Pray earnestly and when I give the signal, go in order, without noise to the doors, Follow Sergeant Harrigan. He will lead us to a place of safety."

"Jail? We going to jail?" some of the older children asked, fear in their voices.

"Yes," Ursula called out. "The jail is strong. It will keep you safe. Along with the policemen. Men like Sergeant Harrigan, children, who has always treated you kindly, has he not?"

"Yes, Ma'am. Yes, Missus," they answered.

The shouts and jeers from above grew louder. Ursula scanned the children's faces. Tears were streaming down their cheeks, but they were ready. She nodded to the police sergeant who doted on the children, and was now ready to shepherd them out.

Still she stood in the doorway after she had counted them all into the alleyway. Sergeant Harrigan took her arm.

"All out and safe, Mrs. Major. I have called you a cab, see it at the end of the street? You must go home now, and guard your own."

"My—?

"Your people of color, Ma'am. You must get them away. Off this island, as we will transport these little ones when it is safe to do so. Under guard, I promise you. We have made space for all at the police station. Please Mrs. Major, get in the carriage. Get off the streets. The ones on the East Side, they have no defense, no single neighborhood to barricade, do you understand me? They will be accosted, one by one. They will be brought down."

"Sergeant Harrigan. How do you know this? And why do you love them?"

"Because they are my own, dear lady. My sister married a sailor, a good man. Two of your little teacher seamstresses? They are my nieces. Now, get your people in the ferries to Brooklyn if you can. If you cannot, hide them. Hide them deep in your cellar. The war has come to our city, Ma'am."

Chapter 50

4th day of the Draft Riots
July 16, 1863
New York City

Rowan understood desperate people. He understood the rich pitting the freed black men and the Irish poor against each other. But he did not understand this: men hanging from lamp posts, burned alive. He thought of Silas and Aaron, back in Pennsylvania, still cooking for and tending their wounded, and was glad they were spared the sight.

He looked up past the bodies and into a sky dark from days of burning, then back at his soldiers. Cinders clung to their clothes. Rowan remembered how much could be endured from his parents, as weak as they were, carrying himself and Talitha up the gangplank of the coffin ship. His men's eyes now looked like theirs, red-rimmed and exhausted. They had caught some sleep on the train that brought them from their Gettysburg camp. Now they were part of the force assigned to put down the riots that had engulfed large parts of the city of New York.

"We must leave these to heaven," Captain Merritt said quietly. "Move on, men."

Company D and its Howitzer cannon had been cut off from the main force, and were now, with remnants of other companies, improvising their way through city streets. It was just as well. This was like no other field of conflict they had known. The blood-curdling yells in the distance were familiar, and the smoke of discharged weapons. But it was no battle. It was a hunt, by packs of Rowan's fellow Irishmen and women, pulling down people they had walked among, worked beside, drank with. Slow moving, street to street. Snipers abounded.

Captain Merritt led them to an abandoned building's stairwell. "Gentlemen, let us survey our surroundings," he said.

Jonathan took hold of his shoulder. "Well, kin. You can finally show me your famed city."

Rowan smiled. How had Ursula's brother maintained his lightness of being after all they had seen, endured? He was loathe to admit it to the preening peacock himself, but Jonathan Kingsley had proven himself a great treasure to Company D. How did his brother-in-law fit himself in everywhere, while remaining apart? No matter. Rowan was glad of it, for his sanguine nature was a boon to his fellow soldiers. He should write that down. Write it for Ursula. It might bring her joy.

The three of them: Rowan, Jonathan, and Captain Merritt, the highest ranking officers, climbed the first three floors of the townhouse and found their way to the balcony. Captain Merritt surveyed their surroundings.

"We cannot allow confrontations on these narrow side streets," he said.

"We would be penned in and trampled."

"Exactly. Whereas, if each of you take a flanking party of fifty men up each of these parallel side streets, on the right and the left, I, with our remaining men and our Howitzer, can press forward. Do we all have a good understanding of this plan?"

Rowan and Jonathan looked to each other and nodded.

"We do, sir."

"Good. Let's hope they disperse. But if they turn on us, we must shoot. Do you understand?"

"Yes, sir."

Rowan did not like having Jonathan out of his sight lines, but there was no helping it, so he tried to clear his mind towards one purpose. They had their duty. But there was no telling what the rioters would do.

He spotted group of six below them, chasing a bloodied black man with a loaf of bread tucked under his arm.

"There's one! Lincoln's ape, Lincoln's monkey, we're coming for you!" they shouted.

Driving away the gang and incorporating the bloodied man deep within their ranks became their next task of the day.

* * *

Rowan took out his penny whistle found a lively tune to hasten the march and make his men think of something other than the chaos and destruction around them. But soon they were halted by a group of a dozen rioters kicking and clubbing at a sack of something in front of a looted dry goods store. Rowan stepped up his penny whistle march to double time. The rioters dispersed, clearing their way.

No, it was not a sack, there on the blue stone sidewalk. It was a man in a police uniform stained with blood. He was wheezing, chest crushed in by the force of the blows.

Rowan knelt beside him.

"Was that "Toss the Feathers?" the man asked.

"It was indeed."

"You're of Connaught, then?"

"Aye, sir. Born in Ballinamore."

"I'm out of Galway Bay. Thanks, my brother, for playing me home."

Rowan's breath caught in the back of his throat. "Is there anything else I can do?"

"Toward Gramercy, you're going?"

Rowan looked up at his commanding officer, who nodded. "Aye."

"Find her. They know her deeds. They'll be hunting her down, too. I sent her home, thought she would be safe. But it has grown worse. Our own, such savagery, brother! She has the heart of a lion, that one. Not stiff-necked righteous, like some of these Protestant abolitionists. It is beyond duty, for the lass. She loves them. You must find her, protect her."

Rowan felt a thrumming in his ears. "Who is that, sir?"

"She found the young ones jobs, got them apprenticed in, around Gramercy Park, where she lives. She will not abandon them. She'll get them out, or hidden. She will abandon none of those children."

Rowan felt his veins ignite. "And this lady's name, sir?"

"Mrs. Major. Her given name I never dared ask, to be sure. But the children know it. And I heard the orphans' matron say it once. Ursula. Ursula Major." He smiled. "Almost a constellation."

The policeman's eyes closed.

The bugle sounded to summon them to their next posting. The Howitzer cannon was ready, hitched to two abandoned horses, by Jonathan, so good with the horses.

Chapter 51

"I am well, only tired," she had promised, there at the ferry. "Go, now."

She did not like lying to Miriam. But Ursula could see no other way. Their lives were intertwined since her own birth. Intertwined unjustly, unequally. Now that Miriam had found her way back to her son, Sling had given her a family again. And the shy Mr. Bell held out the promise of new love. Her dear companion's story must not end. Not here, not with her, whose family had owned Miriam's for generations.

So she had seen them all off for Brooklyn as her pains began. Only Captain Badeau's servant had refused to leave. Ursula pulled Edwin Booth aside. "You must secure him in your cellar, sir. If the mob comes, they will search him out. If they find him, they will kill him. Promise me."

He had, and she trusted him.

Now, in her quiet bedroom, dressed only in her best nightgown and the red silk robe gift from Captain Kane, the pains were coming closer, devouring her. She paced through one, knelt beside her bed for another, paced again, not daring to open a window, even for fresh air. Abandoned. The house must seem abandoned, deserted, locked up against the looters.

She had labored before, had earned Sister Raphaela's respect through her travails. She had a full woman's body now, not a child's, unable to hold what she was holding now, a nine month child. Not hold, no. She must let the child go. The pains were regular, rising in intensity, but the baby was still sitting high.

Come out, little one, it is time. But Ursula had not expected to do any of this alone.

She thought of her daughter, the short breaths of life that had earned her Sister Raphaela's drops of water baptism. Tiny fingers, toes. Did they move? Did life ever reach them? Ursula now had knowledge, and experience, and a womb that knew what to do for this child started by love, not unspeakable violence.

She could bear the pains in silence, but she could not banish the loneliness, the longing for women, both ghosts and the living. For Raphaela, for her mother, for Miriam, safe with her family at their Brooklyn farm, for Madame Picard and for her sister Maries, still willing to welcome her to Canada.

Pounding, below, at the front door. She had been so quiet, sequestering herself away here, not even peering out the windows. Who had betrayed her? More pounding. The door bursting open. Then trampling, footfalls. Heavy, men's footfalls, but no shouts or ugly words that she no longer mistook for a street festival's joy. Perhaps white people were granted this privilege of not being mocked before their homes were pillaged, their lives taken by the madness of the mob. She found Captain Kane's pistol, and put his careful training to shame as she stood by the bed, holding it between her shaking hands.

The door opened. To reveal her brother, his Zouave uniform barely visible through the dirt.

"Put that down," he ordered, grinning. "I'll fetch you the man who deserves it. She's found!" he shouted behind him. "Rowan! Up here!"

Then the two men she loved best in the world stood in her bedroom doorway. The baby dropped, it seemed, to her knees. She felt a whoosh, heard a splash on the floorboards.

"Get in here," she called reaching for the poster and climbing into the bed, "Help me!"

But they remained frozen until their captain came up behind them.

"Well, you war-hardened soldiers. Do what the lady says! The rest of us will secure the premises." He shoved them into the room and closed the door.

Then her husband, sooted like a chimney sweep, climbed onto the bed beside her, holding her face, kissing her deep and long.

"Mind the bruise at her cheek, kin. Looks like my sister has learned some fisticuffs while she's become a New York City street tough."

But Rowan, her eloquent, beautiful Rowan, took only enough time to draw breath before he kissed her again. Yes, yes, that was quite effective.

"Almost done," she managed to say between breaths. "And Miriam has provided."

"Provided what? her brother asked. "I hope she's left us some food."

"Food?" She laughed. "After!"

Rowan stroked the tears from her cheeks. "After what, my darling?"

"You two will need to assist. Jonathan! Wash your hands, now!"

"Without my own kiss from you? It is a good thing I'm used to taking orders from the likes of him," he muttered.

"Scrub! Another is starting."

"Another—?" Rowan began, but stopped abruptly when she dug her nails into his shoulder. "You, husband! Against the bolster, get behind me. Hold me higher."

"Sula, are you unwell?"

The pain subsided. She smiled. "I am quite well. And ready to welcome our child into this awful world."

Jonathan looked up from his place at the water basin. His hands shook. "Oh, no. You cannot do this to us!"

"I do not have a choice in the matter."

"Where is Miriam?" he demanded. "We must find Miriam."

"Miriam's across the river with her family."

"We are her family! Ursula," he looked at the closed bedroom door, "I cannot, we cannot—"

"Steady, soldier," Rowan warned in his best sergeant voice.

"Of course we can," Ursula joined her husband's encouragement, loving the feel of him all around her on the bed. "Miriam has left everything ready, see? Coat off, pull back your sleeves, soldier," she directed at her brother. "Your incessant matchmaking got us into this predicament! The baby and I have the harrrrd parrr—"

She became stuck on her r's and the sound ground its way, long and low between her teeth, down her throat, pressing down, pushing. It felt wonderful. She focused on Rowan's arms, their beautiful braided sleeves. How she loved those arms, those hands, clutching hers, muddying them with sweat.

There, an end to the urging at last. And her brother, her beautiful brother, standing steady.

"There. Now, fold a fresh coverlette under me, and have a look."

Jonathan grumbled quietly, but went about his tasks until Ursula heard his breath catch. "Oh, sister," he whispered.

"What? What do you see?" But the urge was upon her again and she pushed back unto the impenetrable wall that was her husband's chest. Something moved between her legs, something very large. Then, at last, relief.

"Head," Jonathan announced quietly. "Turning. And now, one shoulder and yes, the other. How clever you are, sister. And what a very clever child. What should I—?"

"Hands at the ready," Rowan ordered, "I expect the rest will be coming directly." he kissed her shoulder. "Yes, doctor wife?"

She laughed, pushed, and it did, in a whoosh of fluid.

"Caught, you slippery little rascal!" her brother proclaimed holding up a squirming infant between his hands. He was answered by two gasps of air and an indignant wail.

Ursula glanced quickly up at her husband, squeezing their joined hands. "Oh. Oh, Rowan, look!"

Her brother placed the child gently into their waiting arms. "Now I have a whole roomful of commanding officers," he groused. "Little general, meet your parents," he instructed, "While I find—"

"Second shelf down," Ursula directed.

"…another blanket."

Once tented, the baby's cries became smaller gasps of need. Ursula opened the buttons of her nightgown. The baby dug in closer against her breast and began to suckle.

Ursula looked to Rowan. His glass eye gleamed as the other clouded over with tears.

"What shall we call him?" she asked.

"After your father?"

"Yes! Splendid! And yours. But my darling, I'm afraid I do not know—"

"Nor I, yours."

"Henry."

"Ryan."

"Henry Ryan Buckley," Rowan whispered, "may strong arms hold you, caring hearts tend you, and love await your every step."

When Captain Merritt opened the door, saying, "The area from here to the river is secure and—" his eyes went wide. "Oh, my. You two continue to keep Company D interesting. Reinforcements have arrived. And we have escorted this lady from the docks at her insistence." Miriam slipped in under his arm as he laughed. "Well, Mrs. Henson, it appears there is a new member of your household who did not use a door to arrive."

Miriam planted her fists at her waist. "Still work to do! All men, out!" she proclaimed, before looking past Rowan and Jonathan's bloodied hands, to their faces. "Lieutenant Buckley. Master Jon. All praise to Jesus. God bless you, sirs."

"He has indeed," Rowan said softly.

"I washed my hands, Miriam," Jonathan offered. "Rowan did not."

"Do so again, sirs, now. Then, downstairs to the kitchen, boil up some water, if you would. I shall help Miss

Ursula deliver the afterbirth and then she will need a cup of tea. These two will be presentable upon your return."

* * *

The next morning, Rowan had soothed the baby to sleep with a penny whistle lullaby when their first guests arrived. Asia and her younger brother held arms full of flowers from Ursula's garden. "Rescued from the tramping feet of our army rescuers," Asia said.

Edwin held a curious Edwina in his arms.

"Are these your famed soldier midwives, Mrs. Major?" John Wilkes asked.

Ursula's smile disappeared. "Yes," she said quietly. "Mrs. Clark, Edwin, Edwina, and John Wilkes Booth, may I present Sergeant Kingsley and…" her breath caught with the look on Rowan's face, "and his commanding officer, Lieutenant Buckley."

"A distinct and rousing pleasure, sirs!" Edwin proclaimed, offering his hand to each man flanking her on the bed.

His brother bowed formally. "The curfew has ended. All is well. You need not hover, gentlemen. Feel free to return to your encampment knowing that our neighbor and her son will have their every need met."

"Johnny," Asia admonished. "An orphaned child can never have too many godparents."

Edwin held his daughter higher in his arms. "We have just come from seeing our dear Captain Badeau off to complete his recovery with his family on Rhode Island. His negro man stayed hidden in our cellar as you commanded, dear lady. We tended our friend's wound ourselves, and Ad survived our ministrations, imagine! So, you see, we had our own, lesser adventure!"

Asia's skirts swept against the bedpost. "May we have a look?" she asked.

Ursula lifted the blanket to reveal the sleeping baby.

"What a fine, ruddy child! Does he favor his father?"

237

Ursula stole a quick, pained glance at Rowan. "He does, yes." She searched for his hand beneath the covers, found it, held tight, hating the deception, wishing her guests would leave.

Edwin brought Edwina closer. "Look, a playmate for you soon, darling."

The End

More by Eileen Charbonneau from BWL Publishing, Inc.

American Civil War Brides: Book 1
Seven Aprils

The Code Talker Chronicles
Book 1: I'll Be Seeing You
Book2: Watch Over Me

Eileen Charbonneau is the author of the multiple award-winning historical novels for adults and young people. Her stories explore America through eyes seldom put front and center: her immigrants, her native peoples, her women. Eileen's books have been praised by Kirkus, Library Journal, Publishers Weekly, Booklist, The Washington Post, Boston Globe and many others. She runs a small bed and breakfast inn with her husband in the brave little state of Vermont. Eileen enjoys maple creemies, period dramas and American roots music.

Author's Note

My friend Paulinus Healy, chaplain of the Toronto, Canada Airport, first told me the infinitely sad story of the fallen of Grosse Isle and the wonderfully redemptive one of the French Canadian families who took the Irish orphans into their homes and hearts. "You'll write about it someday," Paulinus predicted. I hope I have captured the great character of fallen people like Rowan and Ursula, who, if shown kindness, return mercy to the world exponentially. Paulinus died after a beautiful life and years of service, devotion, and deep friendships with people all over the world. I hope he would have enjoyed this story.

Many fellow storytellers, writers, readers and fine editors had a hand in my writing life over the years. I am profoundly grateful. Among them are Judith Pittman, Janet Lane Waters, Deborah Barnhart, Yolanda Sly, Eileen O'Finlan, Liz Matis, Sunny Hogg, Ed Renahan, Claire Ruane, Mary Bloxsom, Robert Crooke, Jenna Kernan, Gianna Simonne, Kathy Attalla, Nina Shengold, Juilene Osborne-McKnight, Mark Schoen, Liz Armstrong, Natalia Aponte, Victoria Lea, Susan Wallach, Charlie Rineheimer, Mitzi Flyte, Nancy Bell, Andrea Peterson, Jane Seiver, Tim Bentler-Jungr, Jennifer Probst, Susan King, Janet Evanovich, Cindy Skaggs, Mariah Stewart, Chér Coen, Judy Fitzwater, Nicole Quinn, Cathy Maxwell, Sarah Johnson, Minette Gunther, Andrea Sadler, Yvonne Pinney, Rosemary Morris, Bill Lockwood, Kathleen Gilles Seidel, Jonathan Kruk, Stephanie Cowell, Kathryn Anderson, Denise McInerney, Cindi Myers, Robyn Amos Pope, Laurie Treacy, Dennis Yerry, Anita Gordon, K.I. Going, Evan Pritchard, Joe Bruchac, Joanna Withey, Mary Lenaburg, Maureen Morrison, Jo-Ann Power, Pamela Manché Pearce, Dee Oiler, Wanda Shapiro, Pam Palmer, Eileen Nauman.

I have a special love and appreciation for local booksellers and libraries and all they do for authors and readers. We have great ones in Célina and crew at the Rockingham Public Library and Pat, Alan and Myles at Village Square Booksellers here in Bellows Falls, Vermont.